THE MASTER SHARK'S MATE

FIRE & RESCUE SHIFTERS 5

ZOE CHANT

Copyright Zoe Chant 2017
All Rights Reserved

Created with Vellum

The Fire & Rescue Shifters series

Firefighter Dragon
Firefighter Pegasus
Firefighter Griffin
Firefighter Sea Dragon
The Master Shark's Mate
Firefighter Unicorn

Fire & Rescue Shifters Collection 1
(contains Firefighter Dragon, Firefighter Pegasus, and Firefighter Griffin)

All books in the Fire & Rescue Shifters series are standalone romances, each focusing on a new couple, with no cliff-hangers. They can be read in any order. However, characters from previous books reappear in later stories, so reading in series order is recommended for maximum enjoyment!

CHAPTER 1

"A vacation," the Master Shark said, flatly.

"Yes, a vacation." Neridia, the Pearl Empress, Queen of Atlantis, Commander of Waves and Tides, and Ruler of all the Shifters of the Sea, jabbed one imperial finger in his direction. "I want you to take some time off."

The Master Shark furrowed his brow. For the life of him, he couldn't think what he could possibly have done to have caused such offense. "Your Imperial Majesty, if I have failed you in your absence-"

"Actually, I do need to talk to you about how you've been running things while I was attending to matters on land." The Empress sat up straighter on the Pearl Throne, fixing him with a stern look. "Just today, I've received no fewer than eighteen petitions from the other underwater lords to have you permanently removed from your duties as Voice of the Empress. And from the Sea Council, and in fact from Atlantis itself. A few have even suggested that you should be banished from the ocean entirely. You *have* ruffled their gills, haven't you?"

Long decades of discipline kept his face as impassive as stone, but unease twisted his stomach. The Pearl Empress had spent the better part of her life on land, and had only recently reclaimed her rightful place in the underwater realm of Atlantis. He had played his own part in helping her take the Pearl Throne, and had thought he'd won her trust.

But sharks were misunderstood and feared by every other type of sea shifter — and he was the Master Shark, the most powerful of his kind. The other lords of the Sea Council had to heed him, out of fear of his wrath, but they also hated him. If the Empress had been listening to them…

If she dismisses me, who will keep the peace under the sea? Who will protect the weak and voiceless from the greedy and powerful?

"I'm teasing you." The Empress's stern manner fell away, her full lips curving in a warm smile. "You've been doing marvelously, Master Shark, hunting out the corruption in the Sea Council. I couldn't ask for a better second-in-command, my Voice."

"Then why am I being punished?" he asked, bewildered.

Beside the Pearl Throne, the Empress's Champion and Royal Consort cleared his throat. "I believe Her Imperial Majesty considers this a reward, Master Shark."

The Master Shark exchanged a glance with the Royal Consort. The towering, indigo-haired sea dragon shifter raised one armored shoulder slightly, in a *damned if I know either* gesture of silent sympathy.

The Master Shark turned back to his Empress. "I do not need any rewards. Being able to serve the Pearl Throne is honor enough."

"Master Shark, you've been serving the Empire with unswerving dedication for over thirty years," the Empress said. "Have you *ever* taken a vacation in your entire life? Do you even know what one is?"

"I am fully aware of the concept of vacations," he said, a little stiffly. "I enjoyed many of them with your father, the late Pearl Emperor."

The Empress sighed. "I mean a *real* vacation. Something relaxing. Not battling sea monsters in the depths of the abyss."

Battling sea monsters in the depths of the abyss sounded perfectly relaxing to *him*. Lost for words, he fell back on his usual tactic of staring in silent menace. It worked in most situations.

Not, unfortunately, in this one.

"You are going to take a vacation, Master Shark," the Empress said firmly. "A real vacation. On a beach. Drinking silly cocktails with little paper umbrellas."

He was definitely being punished.

"In fact, I've already booked one for you." The Empress sat back in the gleaming white curves of her throne, looking very pleased with herself. "Don't worry, it's a shifter-only resort. You'll blend right in."

Considering that he was either seven feet tall or eighty feet long depending what form he was in, he could not help but feel that this was wildly optimistic. Even in the underwater city of Atlantis, surrounded by sea dragon shifters, he didn't *blend in*. The only place he might possibly pass unnoticed was the Jurassic era.

"You are going to spend a nice relaxing week sitting on a beach, and doubtless hate every moment of it." The Empress cast him a not unsympathetic look. "But I'm afraid I really do need you to be away from the ocean for a bit. The Sea Council isn't used to me yet. I need to have space to assert my authority, without them constantly looking at you for confirmation."

"Ah." His taut shoulders eased down a little as he finally understood the political undercurrents. "I see."

"I thought you would. You've done a little *too* good a job terrorizing the Sea Council into obedience, my Voice. I need them to get used to listening to me directly now." Neridia lifted her chin, looking uncannily like her late father for a moment, and the Master Shark felt an unaccustomed pang somewhere in the vicinity of his heart. "So. You are going on vacation to Shifting Sands Resort. Just for one week. That's an Imperial order."

The Master Shark could only go to one knee, bowing to her will. "As you command, my Empress."

In his long service to the Pearl Throne, he'd fought krakens, dragons, and even human submarines. He'd united his people and brought them into the Pearl Empire, ending millennia of war between sharks and dragons. With muscle and teeth, cunning and guile, he'd wrestled victory out of the steepest odds.

One week in a land-shifter resort. I can do this. For my Empress.

The Empress fixed him with her penetrating, sea-deep eyes. "And Master Shark? *Relax.* On your honor, promise me that you'll at least try to have fun."

There was no doubt about it. Out of all the services he'd performed for the Pearl Throne over the decades…this was going to be the worst.

CHAPTER 2

"Wait, I'm getting something…" Hitching her sarong up around her knees, Martha Hernandez clambered up onto one of the tables on the terrace overlooking the pool. Heedless of the curious glances she was getting from the other resort guests, she rotated on the spot, methodically waving her cellphone.

She let out a little yip of triumph as the signal strength flickered from one to two bars. "There! Nita, can you hear me? Hello? Nita!"

From the silence on the other side of the line, Martha was somewhat suspicious that her eldest daughter was considering pretending to be going through a tunnel. Unfortunately, the sounds of Manny and Ximena yelling in the background about wanting popsicles rather gave the game away.

"Tell Ximena there *are* orange ones, she just needs to look further back in the big freezer," Martha instructed. "And don't let Manny have one of the grape ones unless he takes his shirt off first. Those stains just do not come out. Oh! That reminds me, make sure you find an excuse to go over to Roddie's tonight. Sniff through his laundry for any hint that he's been fighting the rattlesnakes again. If he crosses the territory line one more time, we're going to have-"

A deep, aggravated sigh crackled over the phone. "Ma, you are meant to be on *vacation*."

The muscle-bound bear shifter behind the bar was eyeballing her as if wondering whether she'd escaped from a secure facility. Martha gave him her best *mind-your-own-business-young-man* glare over the top of her sunglasses.

"What, being on vacation means I can't check up on my family?" Martha said into the phone. "I just want to make sure everything's still all right."

"Everything is *fine*, Ma. Just as it was three hours ago when you last called. Will you please just go and relax?"

"Abuela! Abuela!" Ximena yelled from the background. "Manny took the last orange pop! I'm older, tell him he has to give it to me!"

"No! No!" Manny shrieked. "Mine!"

"Oh dear." Martha clicked her tongue as her grandkids' howls of outrage shifted into *literal* howls of outrage. "Put me on speaker, Nita, before someone starts bleeding."

"No, Ma," her daughter said, with unaccustomed firmness. "You left me as acting alpha. And anyway, they're *my* kids. I'll sort them out. *You* are going to enjoy your nice relaxing vacation."

"I will, honey, I promise. But first just let me–"

"*No,* Ma. And stop calling home. Do you want us all to think you aren't enjoying your present? The one that the whole family saved up *specially* to buy for you, for months and months?"

Part of Martha felt a stab of guilt. The larger part felt admiration at the surgically-precise way her daughter had wielded that edged hint of disappointment.

Maybe she can handle the whole pack in my absence after all.

The thought gave her an odd lump in her throat. She was proud of her daughter for stepping up to the role of acting alpha in her absence, of course…but what if Nita handled it *too* well?

What if they don't really need me anymore?

Martha swallowed, forcing brightness into her tone. "Oh, I'm having a wonderful time here. Tell everyone that it's the best birthday present ever."

"I will, Ma. Now, you go have a good time. And *don't call again.*"

"Love you," Martha said, but the line had already gone dead.

Why has the pack forced us out? Her inner coyote whined forlornly. *Do they think we are too old to hunt? Do they think we can no longer provide for the cubs?*

"Now, that's just being silly," Martha told her animal, trying to convince herself. "Nobody's been outcast. We'll be heading home in a week, and everything will be back to normal."

"Uh, ma'am?" The bartender had approached her table cautiously, as though worried she might bite. "Do you need any help down from there?"

"Nonsense, young man. I'm perfectly capable, thank you." Martha descended from her perch with as much stately dignity as could be mustered while wearing a swimsuit and sarong. "There, see? I don't need your help."

His rugged, handsome face crooked in a wry grin. "I can see that, ma'am. But I do think you could use one of my margaritas, if you don't mind me sayin'."

"What a nice boy you are." Martha patted his arm—goodness, it was like petting a rock—and sank down onto a deckchair. She gusted out a sigh. "Better make it two. Big ones."

"Yes, ma'am." With a respectful tip of his hat, the bartender went off to make the drinks.

Martha stared down at the sparkling turquoise pool, idly kicking the toes of her flip-flops together. "Relax," she muttered. "Enjoy myself. Don't worry about home. Right. Easy."

It *should* have been easy. Shifting Sands was a beautiful place. Just off the coast of Costa Rica, the private island was like a jewel cupped in the hand of the sea. And the whole place was just for shifters. Not a single human in the entire resort, or indeed the entire island.

No need to worry about secrecy. No need to worry about protecting her family from hunters, or keeping the rambunctious pack in line. No chores to be done, no mouths to feed, no babies to soothe.

For the first time in longer than she could remember, Martha was completely free to do whatever she wanted.

If she could just work out what that was.

She signed again, tucking her cellphone back into her beach bag. She retrieved the resort pamphlet from the side pocket, flipping through it.

Shifting Sands offered a mind-boggling array of entertainments. She could go out whale-watching in the resort boat. She could learn to snorkel. She could get a massage in the spa, hike through the jungle, take a day trip to the mainland to sightsee... there was even a salsa dance tomorrow evening.

So many diversions... and no-one to share them with her.

Dropping the pamphlet, she watched the gentle sway of the palms lining the pool. Without conscious thought, she found herself rubbing the old, worn gold band of her wedding ring.

Miss you, Manuel.

Ten years of widowhood had worn the sharp stab of loss down, of course. But something about this peaceful tropical paradise made her long once again for his bright, ready smile and laughing eyes.

The warm breeze whispered over her bare arms like a lover's caress. If Manuel had been with her now, she knew *exactly* what they'd be doing.

Oh, how I miss a man's touch.

She snorted at the ridiculous thought. She was a respectable widow, and a grandma to boot. That part of her life was long gone.

Movement caught the corner of her eye. Thinking it was the bartender coming back with her drink—or drinks—she sat up, twisting around.

"Holy Mother of God!" She jumped so hard that she nearly fell off her deckchair.

It wasn't the burly bartender. *This* man looked like he might have eaten the bartender for breakfast, possibly washed down with a few gallons of protein shake. He wasn't so much built as constructed.

Her eyes tracked upward of their own accord, past hard thighs bigger than her head and eight-pack abs. He wore nothing but black swimming shorts, leaving the apparently endless expanse of his muscular chest on full display. His skin was so pale he looked like a sculpture carved from marble, marred by the faint lines of old, criss-crossed scars.

Pack leader though she was, the man exuded such an aura of dominance that he had her inner coyote rolling onto its back instantly. Whoever—or whatever—he was, there was no doubting his power.

Martha's heart thudded against her ribs. Her own alpha coyote had never once, in all her years, submitted to another shifter's animal...

Wait.

Her coyote wasn't rolling in submission. For all the man's hulking physical strength and overwhelming presence, she didn't feel the slightest bit afraid of him.

No, her coyote was whining and writhing in...*invitation.*

"Oh," Martha breathed.

He was so tall, she couldn't see his face until he tipped his head down. He had the most striking features she'd ever seen—not conventionally handsome, with his heavy brow and wide jaw, but arresting. A strong will had shaped those weathered lines, over long, difficult years. His iron-gray hair was sheared brutally short, like an army recruit's. There was something military too about his perfectly still, straight-backed stance.

His deep-set eyes met hers. They were as gray as his hair, hard as tempered steel.

"You," he rasped.

"Oh no." Martha scrabbled off the side of the deckchair, heedless of dignity. "Nope, nope, nope."

The man's impassive expression never changed. Not an eyelid flickered, not a muscle twitched.

"No!" Martha yelped, and fled from her one true mate.

CHAPTER 3

*N*aturally, she ran away from him.

Sharks rarely had true mates. They were too independent, too individualistic, for such pair-bonding. Brief, fierce liaisons, fleeting moments of contact in a life of silent, solitary wandering—that was the way of sharks.

And he was the Master Shark. He was *the* shark. The heart and soul of his people.

No wonder his mate had taken one look at him, and shown him her heels.

"Hey."

He couldn't tear his eyes away from his mate's retreating back. So little, so soft, yet so swift and fierce. Brown and ripened by a lifetime spent under open, cloudless skies. She smelled of things he'd never known: sun-warmed fur and long summer days, dry desert winds and laughter rising to the moon.

"Hey," the bartender said again from behind him. "Is there some sort of problem here…*sir?*"

His mate had disappeared behind a concealing wall of greenery. The Master Shark turned at last, looking down at the bartender. To his credit, the bear shifter didn't back down, although his feet set in a defensive stance.

"No," he told the bartender, flatly.

"Begging your pardon, that's not what it looks like to me." The bear shifter held a large, iced drink in each hand, and looked fully prepared to employ them as weapons if necessary. "What did you do to make her run off like her tail was on fire?"

The Master Shark stared at him, silently.

"I guess that answers that question," the bartender muttered. He raised his voice again, meeting the Master Shark's eyes without flinching. "Look, I know who you are, and honestly, I don't care. You can't go around terrorizing other guests."

He was well-used to other shifters treating him with suspicion. It was inevitable, given what he was. Nonetheless, his back stiffened at the inadvertent accusation that he might ever even *think* of threatening his mate.

"That was not my intention," he said coldly. "I merely wished to…"

He stalled, words drying in his throat. What *had* he intended?

He didn't know himself. All he'd known was that the instant he'd set foot on the island, he'd been pulled by a blood-scent more compelling than any he'd ever known. He could no more *not* have followed that siren call than he could stop swimming.

And he had found *her*. And she had fled from him.

The bartender grimaced, his tense body language relaxing a bit. "Well, whatever you intended, clearly all you succeeded in doing was terrifying that nice lady. I think it would be better if you just left her alone from now on, okay?"

"She is my mate."

The bear shifter's mouth hung open for a second. "No shit?"

"No," the Master Shark looked back in the direction his mate had vanished, "as you say, shit."

The bartender digested this for a moment. Then he handed him one of the drinks. "Here. I think you're going to need this."

The Master Shark sniffed cautiously at the alarmingly-colored beverage. "Alcohol?"

"Sure is. Uh, don't you have booze under the sea?"

He shook his head, putting the glass down untouched. "The deeps are not a place for dulled wits. Only the suicidal would deliberately impair themselves."

"Guess I can rule Atlantis out of my list of job opportunities." The bartender stuck out a hand. "Tex. Never met a shark before. Or royalty, for that matter."

The Master Shark regarded the proffered hand, then shook it carefully. "I am not royalty. Not for many decades. Now, I am merely the Empress's Voice."

"Not sure the word 'merely' belongs in that sentence." Tex tipped his head a little to one side, studying him. "So. You and her. Really?"

He lifted one shoulder fractionally. "It appears so."

Tex let out a low whistle. "And I thought I was unlucky in love. Well, assuming you're going to try again, I've got a friendly piece of advice for you. Up here on land, we have this thing called 'smiling.' You might try it some time."

The Master Shark did so.

"Sweet daisies," Tex muttered, taking a half-step back. "On second thought, definitely don't do that. Maybe you could just…loom less. Somehow."

He looked down at himself. He looked back at Tex, who was large for a land shifter, but still at least six inches under his own height. Words seemed unnecessary.

"Yeah, okay." Tex scratched the back of his neck, eying him rather dubiously. "Y'know, I've seen some odd couples in my years behind the bar, but this one sure beats all. A coyote and a shark? Not exactly a natural match, I hope you don't mind me saying."

The Master Shark's jaw tightened, but privately he had to admit that the bear shifter had a point. His mate—his *mate!*—was clearly a creature of the desert, while he could count on the fingers of one hand the number of times in his long life he had ever ventured onto dry land. Fate clearly had a sense of humor worthy of a human.

Nonetheless, the inescapable fact remained. She was his mate.

To be a shark was to be driven by an unfillable void. He had heard other shifters speak sometimes of their inner animals as if they were the other half of their souls, a whisper in their minds. He had never understood what they meant. *His* soul was a silent predator, eternally seeking, never satisfied.

Now, he knew that he had never truly been hungry before. Not compared to this all-consuming need.

He'd had decades of practice at hiding his emotions, but the shock of the encounter had rattled even his control. Something of his thoughts must have shown in his manner, because Tex's eyes softened in sympathy.

"Hey, you'll work it out." The bartender collected the unwanted drink. "So what are you going to do now?"

"What my kind do best." The Master Shark allowed his lips to curl once again, exposing a brief, predatory flash of teeth. "Hunt."

CHAPTER 4

"You thirsty, honey?"

Martha looked up from her waffle, expecting to find a waitress with a pot of coffee. Instead, a vast woman overflowing from a vibrant pink maxi dress gave her a cheeky wink as she put down her own breakfast plate down at Martha's table.

"Because if you are," the woman continued, her voice dropping to a delighted, throaty whisper, "I can't help but notice that there seems to be a tall glass of water with your name on, right over there."

Martha didn't need to look round to know that the man she'd met yesterday—she was *not* going to think of him as her mate—was watching her from the buffet table. Ever since their brief meeting yesterday, she'd been acutely aware of his every movement, even from clear across the resort. It was like she was a fish on his hook; an unbreakable, invisible line connecting them together.

Martha scowled, resolutely keeping her back to him. No matter how much she wanted to sneak a peek to see if he really was as devastatingly charismatic as she remembered, she was *not* going to look round.

Manuel, she reminded herself, touching her thumb to her wedding band. Even though he was with the angels now, he was still her husband. She'd been married to him for thirty good, golden years, along with the inevitable few rocky ones. They'd had kids and raised them well; built a home and filled it with laughter. With all her heart and soul, she'd loved her husband, and the life they'd made together.

What sort of woman would she be if she let her head be turned by some stranger now, just because her coyote was no better than a bitch in heat?

"Oooh, honey." The voluptuous woman's grin widened. "It's obvious you *both* got it bad. Who is he, anyway?"

"No idea," Martha said, slicing a banana rather more viciously than the innocent fruit deserved. "Don't know him."

"I pretty sure he'd like to get to know you. In the Biblical sense, if you take my meaning." The woman winked again, settling her impressive weight into the chair opposite Martha. "I'm Magnolia. This is your first time at Shifting Sands, right?"

Magnolia's smile was so warm and generous, Martha couldn't help but smile back. "Is it that obvious?"

"I know all our regulars. Been here over a year now myself. Something about this island, well…" She glanced sidelong at Martha, sly as a coyote herself. "It makes you feel young again, doesn't it? You can just feel your sap rising."

Martha was pretty sure it wasn't the island that was making *her* sap rise. Even now, the silent, unseen presence behind her was bringing an unfamiliar tingle to certain places best left forgotten.

"I'm a grandma," she said, a touch too primly. "If the Good Lord had wanted my sap to be rising, he would've made me a tree."

"Now, don't go putting yourself in the ground before you're dead." Magnolia leaned to one side a little, looking past Martha. "You want to know what he's doing now?"

She stabbed at her waffle. "Nope."

"Menacing the fruit basket," Magnolia reported anyway. "Does he hold a deep and personal grudge against oranges, or does he just always look like that?"

"Wouldn't know." Her fork screeched across the china plate. "Don't care."

"Well, *I* am just dying of curiosity. Like I said, I know all our regulars, and I can tell you that *he* is not our usual sort of guest." Magnolia fluttered a ringed hand, attracting the attention of the politely unobtrusive waiter hovering nearby. "Breck! Dish me the dirt on that brooding slab of beefcake over there."

Breck—a slim, breathtakingly handsome man who was probably young enough to be Martha's grandson—wagged a reproachful finger. "Now, Magnolia, you know staff aren't allowed to discuss guests." His voice dropped conspiratorially. "And even if we were, I would *not* be discussing *that* one. Certainly not behind his back."

"Why?" Martha asked, drawn despite herself. "Who is he?"

Breck shook his head. "Sorry, ma'am. The boss would have me served up on a platter as the dish of the day if I breathed so much as a word. She's very serious about protecting the privacy of…special guests."

Magnolia looked intrigued. "So he *is* someone important. Well, in that case, guess I'll just have to find out for myself."

"Don't." Breck turned deadly serious, all his flirtatious manner dropping away. "I mean it, Magnolia. Don't go near him."

Magnolia raised her eyebrows. "Well, that's going to be difficult, because he's heading this way."

The waiter stiffened, pasting a professionally blank smile onto his face. "Sir," he said, turning. "Can I help you with that?"

The man looked down at the single plate he was carrying. There was a pineapple on it. A *whole* pineapple.

Who on earth takes the pineapple *from a fruit basket?*

The man contemplated his unusual breakfast for a moment, then switched his stare back to Breck. It was obvious that he was not in need of assistance. Martha suspected he could have comfortably carried *Breck* in one hand, and quite possibly the entire table as well.

Breck made a valiant attempt at rallying, despite the man's cold gaze. "Sir, this table is occupied. Let me find you another one. I have a very nice, private table out on the-"

"No."

The word was spoken with utmost finality. It was clear that this was The Table. There would be no Other Tables. If Other Tables were suggested again, there would be Consequences.

"It's fine," Martha said, before the poor brave waiter got himself killed over dining arrangements. She pushed her barely-touched waffle away. "I was just leaving, anyway."

The man immediately abandoned his pineapple. It was clear that wherever she was going next, he would be going too. His impenetrable gray eyes fixed on her with such unnerving attention, she felt practically stripped naked.

She tore her own eyes away from him, praying that he couldn't smell the sharp leap of her desire. Her immediate thought was to flee to her private cottage again. It was clear that she simply couldn't trust her coyote around this man.

But damn it, her family had scrimped and saved over months in order to surprise her with the vacation of a lifetime. Even five-year-old Manny had contributed a nickel from his allowance every week. When they asked her how her trip had been, what was she going to tell them?

Oh, I just stayed within four walls all day with the curtains drawn, because my fool hormones made me want to bang a total stranger like a screen door in a hurricane.

Her coyote helpfully supplied a very vivid mental picture of exactly what that might be like. Those rough, scarred hands closing around her arms. His irresistible strength lifting her as effortlessly as a leaf in the wind, pinning her against a wall. Wrapping her legs around his waist, his hardness between her thighs-

Martha cleared her throat, mentally sitting on her inner animal. *Down, girl.*

If the stranger had sensed any of her thoughts, he didn't show it. He simply stood there, watching her in silence, patient as an old hound dog.

There has to be somewhere I can go where he can't follow.

Inspiration struck. There *was* one place in the resort where she was absolutely certain a scarred, muscle-bound, red-blooded alpha male like him wouldn't possibly dare to venture.

"I," she announced to the world in general, "am going to the spa."

CHAPTER 5

The Master Shark knew a challenge when he saw one. His life had been evenly divided between war and politics; he was no stranger to struggles for dominance, whether they were fought with teeth or words.

The proud lift of his mate's chin, the fire in her dark eyes, the oh-so-careful way she didn't quite look at him; she was issuing a challenge. Demanding that he prove his strength and worth before she would deign to even acknowledge his presence.

He had never backed down from a challenge. He would win this one too.

Once he figured out what in the sea it could possibly be.

"A pedicure?" the tiny land-shifter woman in charge of the 'spa' repeated, as if she hadn't quite believed him the first time.

"Yes." He had no idea what one was, but from the triumphant note in his mate's voice as she'd ordered her own, she believed that it was something a shark could not do.

He would prove her wrong. He would endure, no matter how she tested him. He would show her that he was more than the blood-blinded animal his reputation made him out to be. He would show her the best of himself; his patience, his persistence. Silently, with actions rather than words, he would destroy the stereotype she projected onto him, so that she could finally see the man underneath the monster.

And when she did, he could only hope that she would not turn away.

The spa attendant made a tiny shrug, as if to say that if he was determined to face the 'pedicure,' on his own head be it. "This way, sir."

She led him through a curtain made of shells strung on thin ropes. He had to bend nearly double in order to fit through the low archway. When he saw what awaited beyond, he immediately understood.

Oh, clever, clever mate. Not a challenge of strength, or endurance. This is a test of softness.

The light, airy room was lined with comfortable wicker chairs draped in pristine white towels. Grooming instruments—for forms both animal and human—hung from the white-washed walls. A sweet, gentle scent hung in the air, drifting up from scattered candles. Wide windows kept the room pleasantly cool and offered soothing views of the sparkling turquoise bay.

It was a place for pampering. A place to be touched gently, by soft clean hands that had never known war. A place of peace and beauty.

No wonder she had thought a shark would not follow her here.

Well, he would show her that even he could enjoy softness. More than anything in the sea, he longed to enjoy *her* softness.

His lips curved a little at the intoxicating thought, but he forced the smile back. Dry-landers did not react well to the sight of a shark's teeth, as Tex the bartender had demonstrated. He schooled his face to impassiveness as the spa attendant led him to a chair.

His mate was enthroned like a queen a few seats down, her own attendant kneeling at her feet as if in supplication. They had been chattering away in some human language he did not know, but broke off at his appearance. They both stared at him as if…well, as if he was a shark. In a koi pond.

"If you please, sir?" His own attendant knelt down, gesturing at him.

Apparently she wanted his feet, though for what purpose still escaped him. He forced his muscles to relax, allowing the tiny woman to do as she pleased.

The spa attendant let out a soft, surprised breath. "No calluses. You have beautiful feet, sir."

He didn't know why she sounded so astonished. It wasn't like he used them much, after all.

The land-shifter woman shook her head ruefully. "To be honest, sir, I'm rather at a loss as to what to do here."

Nonetheless, she reached for some sort of lotion. Spreading it onto her hands, she began to rub his soles.

His mate had gone back to pointedly ignoring him. Pretending indifference, he tipped his head back, closing his eyes. The sensation of firm fingers running over his instep was surprisingly pleasant, once he'd managed to subdue his instinctive urge to kick his assailant in the face.

"I've got five kids," his mate announced.

He cracked open one eye, but she was still pointedly not looking at him. She appeared to be addressing her own attendant. Since she'd chosen to speak in English, however, he was confident that he was the real target of her words.

"Juanita, she's my eldest, she's mated to a lovely jackalope girl, just sweet as pie. They've got two kids of their own. My boy Nic, he and his mate have got one on the way too. Due in September. Can't wait to smell that new-baby scent again. Grandpups are such a blessing."

Ah. Another challenge.

She was indirectly telling him of her wealth—not in the sorts of unimportant trinkets valued by dragons, but *true* wealth. A shark knew that blood was the greatest prize of all. He listened as she so-casually mentioned name after name, treasure after treasure: children and grandchildren, sisters and brothers, nieces and nephews and cousins.

The undercurrent to her words was clear: *I am the matriarch of a vast, powerful clan. What can* you *give me?*

An unaccustomed wave of uncertainty washed over him. He was

the Master Shark, and the Empress's Voice, true. But his wealth was copper to her gold. Though all the sharks of the sea owed him fealty, it was a cold, formal relationship. Nothing compared to the love and loyalty of true family.

What *did* he have to offer her?

Only himself. But a woman as powerful and desirable as her could have her pick of males, as indeed she clearly had done in the past. He was her true mate, yes…but what if land-shifters didn't feel that bond as intensely as the people of the sea did?

A strange, cold feeling gripped his heart. It was an emotion he had not felt in so long, it took him a moment to identify it.

For the first time in decades, he was afraid.

CHAPTER 6

Martha sat on the beach and fumed.

She'd nattered on inanely about her grandkids until the poor girls at the spa had been practically cross-eyed with boredom, and yet *he* still hadn't taken the hint. He was still following her around as if she was some short-skirted cheerleader instead of a respectable grandma. What did she have to do, whip out some needles and start pointedly knitting a scarf at him?

Leave me be! she wanted to yell at her hulking shadow. *Stop making me feel things I've got no business feeling at my time of life!*

But that would involve talking to him. And so far, he still hadn't said more than that single word—"You"—to her.

And there was another thing. If he wasn't going to leave her alone, why in the name of all the saints didn't he just *talk* to her? What was he playing at, following her around in silence like this? He was bad as a tomcat lingering at a door, neither in nor out.

She risked a peek at him, relying on her oversized sunglasses to conceal the direction of her gaze. He'd parked himself a little way down the beach, strong features in profile to her, his face turned toward the sea. Though the private cove was amply provisioned with deckchairs and parasols—not to mention a charming open-fronted hut containing a fully stocked bar—he sat cross-legged and straight-backed directly on the white sand, in the full glare of the scorching midday sun.

Sniff him, her inner coyote said.

"For crying out loud," Martha muttered to herself. "I am *not* going to sniff him, you fool beast."

Her coyote nipped at her mental heels. *Sniff!*

From experience, Martha knew that her animal could be a right pain in the psychic backside when it was in this sort of mood. Rolling her eyes, she gave way to her coyote's insistence. It was either that or be unable to hear herself think for the next two hours.

Martha had always had a good nose, even for a coyote (*a nose for trouble,* her own long-suffering abuela had muttered on more than one occasion). Surreptitiously, she turned her face into the breeze, catching the man's scent.

Oh, dear Lord.

Salt and sea and a fierce, coppery tang that made her knees go weak as a day-old colt. If some fancy perfume house could distill that scent, it would come in jet-black bottles and cost five hundred dollars an ounce. He smelled of pure, primeval power.

And not sunscreen, her coyote pointed out pragmatically.

Martha blinked. Her animal was right. The man had barely a stitch of clothing on, and yet his pale skin gleamed with nothing more than sweat. The damn fool wasn't even wearing a hat.

"Oh, for the love of-" Flinging down her magazine, Martha marched over to the beach hut.

As well as a mini fridge full of drinks, it also contained a basket of complementary beach necessities. She rummaged around until she found a bottle of extra-strength sunscreen. Then, before she could talk herself out of it, she stalked over to the man.

"Here." Ungraciously, she thrust the bottle out at him. "You're white as a fish's belly. You'll burn faster than you can heal, in this sort of sun."

A flicker of something—surprise?—flashed across those storm cloud eyes. He looked at her offering for a moment, not moving a muscle. Then, as carefully as if it was made of spun sugar, he took the bottle.

"Thank you." The deep, dry rasp of his voice made her toes curl involuntarily into the sand.

Martha gave him a curt nod. She'd intended to take her fool self straight back to her deckchair, but something about the way the man held the sunscreen bottle in his huge hands made her pause.

"You do know what to do with that, right?" she asked.

His gaze slid sideways. Though his face remained impassive, Martha had the oddest feeling that he was embarrassed. He didn't say anything.

"You rub it on. Like this." Taking the bottle back from him, Martha shook a good dollop into the palm of her hand.

She'd intended to put it on her own arm in demonstration…but she'd spent forty years sunscreening up wriggling, protesting kids. Out of sheer force of habit, she slapped her palm down onto the man's shoulder.

She froze. He…didn't exactly freeze, seeing as how he'd previously barely been breathing, but he reached a new, practically rock-like state of stillness.

The simple contact reverberated through every inch of body. She felt like the desert blooming under the first touch of rain, new life springing up from dry, dusty ground.

Blushing furiously, she started to pull her hand back—but the man moved first, twisting in a blur of motion too fast to follow. Before she knew what was happening, his hard, callused hand trapped her own, holding it pinned against his skin.

Her breath caught in her throat. His eyes were the barest ring of iron around deep, black pupils, dark and hungry with desire.

The man blinked, once. She could feel his shoulder hitch as he drew a ragged breath. "I…my apologies. I did not mean to frighten you."

"You didn't." Martha's heart was pounding, but it certainly wasn't with fear. She cleared her throat, trying to pretend that they were having a perfectly normal conversation. "I-I'll do your back for you. Can't reach it properly yourself, after all."

Slowly, he released her hand, though he stayed twisted round, watching her out of the corner of his eye.

Avoiding his gaze, she bent to her task. Much as she fought to keep her touch brisk and impersonal, she couldn't help the heat rising in her blood as she smoothed the lotion over the dips and swells of his muscled back.

"I'm Martha," she said, since it seemed rude to be rubbing a man without even introducing herself. "Martha Hernandez."

"Martha." He repeated her name softly, as though tasting it on his tongue.

She waited, but he didn't say anything further. "And you?" she prompted.

He turned his head away, staring out to sea once more. "You know who I am."

Mate, her coyote whispered. *Our mate.*

"Nope," Martha said, stubbornly ignoring her inner animal. "The staff wouldn't tell me."

He whipped back round, staring at her, and she flushed as she realized that she'd inadvertently let on that she'd asked after him. She occupied herself with squirting more sunscreen into her hand, avoiding his eyes.

"You…" he said slowly. "You don't know who I am? *What* I am?"

She shook her head. "Never smelled anything like you before. Couldn't even begin to guess your animal."

His face locked down, impassive as a tombstone.

"You don't have to tell me," she added hastily, though in truth she was eaten up by curiosity. "I know some shifters don't like to share their secrets with just anyone."

He said nothing, for so long that she started to wonder if he was ever going to speak again.

Then, so quietly she barely heard him: "Shark."

No wonder she hadn't recognized his scent. "Huh. Great White?"

"No."

She waited, but apparently that was all he had to say on that topic. "Well, you got a name, or should I just call you Mister Shark?"

He looked away again. "Master."

"What?"

"Master Shark. Not Mister."

She snorted. "If you think I'm calling you *that*, you got another think coming."

He said nothing. His shoulders stiffened in a tense, straight line.

"Wait." Martha stared at the back of his head. "Seriously? You aren't kidding? You're what, the king of the sharks or something?"

"Not king. Not anymore. Just the Master Shark."

Not *anymore*? Implying that he *had* been at some point? Martha's mind reeled.

"If you didn't know…" He still wasn't looking at her, eyes fixed on the horizon. "Why did you run from me?"

Her wedding ring glinted up at her in accusation.

Martha snatched her hands away from his back. She rubbed her greasy palms down her own thighs, wishing she could scrub away the memory of touching him along with the residue of the sunscreen.

She cleared her throat. "There you go. All done."

His massive muscles shifted under his pale, gleaming skin as he turned to face her. She was trapped again by the sheer power behind his iron-gray eyes.

"Why?" he repeated.

He'd been honest with her, even though he'd thought that it would scare her off. She owed him the truth in return.

She held up her left hand, showing him her ring. "I'm already mated."

"No." His voice was flat, utterly certain. "You are not."

"Well, I *was*." His arrogance raised her hackles. "Thirty years we were together. He was loyal to me, and I'm still loyal to him, and that's all there is to it."

He held her glare for a long moment. Then he looked down, absently running a hand over his short, bristling hair. It was the first time she'd ever seen him fidget, or move with less than total confidence. It made him more real, somehow. Her hands ached to reach out to him again.

"Do you need someone killed?" he said abruptly.

Her mouth hung ajar. "*Excuse* me?"

"I cannot fight the dead. Give me a living foe, a way I can serve you. Is there some insult to your honor that demands vengeance?"

Her inner coyote's ears pricked up. *Tell him about the shih tzu that keeps peeing in our yard.*

Martha pinched the bridge of her nose. "Are you out of your fool mind?" she said, to both of them.

"I would fill the sea with blood for you, if you asked." Though his harsh, toneless voice never changed, one corner of his mouth twitched up a fraction, as if he was fully aware of how ridiculous his words were. "But I suspect that you will not."

"You got that right," Martha said firmly. "I don't know what it's like where you come from, but up here on land, we don't go around murdering our way into people's hearts. If you like a lady, you offer her flowers, not a bloodbath."

He glanced at the manicured jungle edging the beach, eyes narrowing.

"That was just a hypothetical example," she added, before he marched off and uprooted a whole shrub. "I don't need any flowers."

One of his hands flexed a little, fingers clenching in the white sand. "Then what do you need?"

"Nothing," Martha said, trying to stop her ears to her coyote's whining. "I had my husband, and no matter what you do to try to impress me, nothing is going to change that. Please, just let me be. I've had love enough in my life, more than anybody could ask for. I've got my memories. I'm content enough."

"I know I am…I am not what you need. Or want." His voice roughened even further, harsh as sandpaper on skin. "But let me do something for you. Anything. Let *me* have a memory, that I once did something that pleased you, and I…I too will try to be content."

Her heart broke for him. It wasn't *his* fault that his one true mate had already been claimed. Life had handed him a whole bushel of lemons, and all he was asking for was one spoonful of sugar.

"All right then. But I don't need anyone murdered, thank you very much." She racked her mind, trying to think of something she could ask him to do for her.

It can't just be some make-work fluff. A man like him needs a task he can be proud of, a real honest-to-God challenge.

If it's a difficult feat he's after... Her coyote's tongue lolled out in a trickster's grin. *There is one thing we could ask him to do.*

Despite herself, her own lips curved as well. "Can you dance?"

CHAPTER 7

The waiter looked at Tex, then back up at the Master Shark. The expression on the small land-shifter's face very clearly stated: *I am going to die.*

"Come on, Breck." Tex twanged an encouraging chord on his guitar. "You've always claimed that you could teach anyone to salsa. Time to put your money where your mouth is."

"You've got the easy job," muttered the other man Tex had summoned, who the bartender had introduced as Travis. He was attempting to measure the span of the Master Shark's arms, which was somewhat difficult in the limited space within the vacation cottage. "We're going to need a bigger tape measure. Tex, there is no way in hell I can adjust a shirt to fit this mons- uh, gentleman. Not by tonight, anyway."

Tex scratched the back of his neck. "What if you started with something of Chef's?"

"I'd have to start with something of *Magnolia's* just to have enough fabric to fit round his chest." Travis cocked a wry eyebrow up at the Master Shark. "And I'm not sure that pink floral would give quite the effect you're looking for, sir."

The Master Shark considered it. "I am not attempting to appear intimidating. Dry-landers consider pink an unthreatening color, do you not?"

Tex, Breck, and Travis gazed at him for a long, wordless moment. Even though they were all different sorts of shifters—and thus shouldn't be capable of communicating telepathically with each other—he had the distinct impression that all three of them were sharing the same mental image.

"The temptation is almost overwhelming," Travis murmured.

"No," Tex said firmly.

"Spoilsport."

"Come on, it's his one true mate. Let's give the poor guy a chance." Tex idly picked out a plaintive, wistful melody on his guitar. "I promised we'd help him out."

"You're a sucker for doomed romance." Travis snapped his tape measure shut with a sigh. "I'm sorry, but there's really nothing I can do. Even I can't pull super-sized formalwear out of my ass at two hours' notice."

The Master Shark tilted his head. "Tonight's dance is a formal occasion?"

Travis shrugged. "Well, it's not white tie or anything, but we do encourage guests to dress up a bit. You're going to need a little more than swim shorts, sir."

"I have formalwear." He pulled open the small wardrobe in demonstration.

There was a small, stunned silence.

"Oh, my tail and whiskers." Breck let out a long, low whistle. "Well, I for one would pay good money to see him wear *that*."

"Yeah, but on a dance floor?" Tex said dubiously.

"I think it'll work." Travis rubbed his chin. "If we lose some of the…accessories."

∽

"Accessories," Magnolia said, pursing her lips in consideration. "You need just a tiny splash of color. Aha! I know the perfect thing."

"Oh, no," Martha protested, as Magnolia plucked a vibrant red hibiscus blossom from the vase on the dresser. "I can't go around putting flowers in my hair like some slip of a girl. I don't want to draw attention to my gray hairs."

"Now, why would you be ashamed of these beautiful silver streaks?" Magnolia put her hand on top of Martha's head, foiling her attempt to duck away. "Hold still."

For a soft-looking person, Magnolia had a grip like a bear trap. Martha could only submit as the other woman carefully pinned the flower behind her left ear.

"There." Magnolia stepped back, admiring her handiwork. "Wonderful. You *shall* go to the ball, Cinderella."

Martha studied herself in the mirror critically. She had to admit, Magnolia's deft touch had worked wonders. Martha would never have dared to use such bold eyeliner, but the smoky tones made her copper-brown eyes look as bright as new pennies. The scarlet hibiscus flower somehow transformed her salt-and-pepper hairdo into something elegant and sophisticated rather than short and sensible.

"You've got real style," she said to Magnolia in admiration. "You can even make an old desert dog look presentable."

"Oh, I don't think I can claim credit for the pink in your cheeks," Magnolia said with a shamelessly lewd wink. "I'm pretty sure that's down to a certain Mr. Tall, Pale, and Sharkish. Now, promise you'll find me at breakfast tomorrow and tell me all the juicy details."

"Won't be anything to tell," Martha said primly as she searched for her shoes amidst the piles of rejected clothes scattered across the floor. "You'll be at the dance, after all. You'll see everything for yourself."

Magnolia let out a rich, throaty chuckle. "You say that now, but you haven't seen *his* outfit yet."

"How on earth would you know what he's wearing?"

Magnolia waggled her eyebrows mysteriously. "My spies are everywhere. Now, I've got to run and meet my own date. I'll drop in at Housekeeping on the way and ask them to come tidy up in here while you're out."

"Oh, don't do that." Magnolia *had* rather torn through Martha's limited wardrobe like an incredibly fashion-conscious tornado, but Martha hardly wanted to be bothering the poor staff at this time of the evening. "I'll sort it out myself later."

"You might be busy later." Magnolia shot her a sly glance over her shoulder as she headed out the door. "And it never hurts to be prepared for visitors. Or rather, *a* visitor."

She disappeared down the path in a flutter of silk before Martha could think of a suitably scathing retort. Growling under her breath, she slipped on her shoes. She hesitated at the door, casting a last glance back at the room.

Maybe I should tidy up just a little.

Shaking her head free of the silly notion, she left the room exactly as it was. The fact that her baggy underthings were on full display meant that she'd have to think twice before issuing any…impulsive invitations. She needed all the help she could get to keep a leash on her fool inner animal. Her coyote was frisking like a pup with anticipation already.

"Settle down, you," she muttered as she closed the door behind herself. "It's just a dance. That's all."

The stars were just starting to gleam in the deep turquoise sky, but the full moon had already climbed high above the horizon. Nightblooming jasmine filled the air with a heady, hypnotic scent. Despite her attempt to rein in her coyote's exuberance, Martha couldn't help feeling practically giddy herself as she followed the curving, whitegraveled path that ran from the guests' cottages to the main part of the resort.

Oh, it's been too long since I last went dancing.

She'd used to go practically every week, before she'd gotten married. But Manuel, bless his soul, had possessed two left feet and the sense of rhythm of a stunned duckling. After the kids had come along, it just didn't feel right to ask him to spend their few precious date nights doing something he hated.

I hope he doesn't hate it. Martha felt a twinge of guilt at her own mischievousness for setting her mate this challenge. *Though he probably will.*

She didn't imagine that a person who didn't even have *feet* most of the time would care for dancing. Or have much experience of it.

Well, it'll serve me right if he breaks all my toes.

Candles in colored glass jars flickered among the tropical shrubs, guiding the way to the main building. The French windows lining the dining room had been folded back for the evening. Her pulse kicked up a notch as a sudden intoxicating roll of samba drums came from inside. A few other couples had already gathered on the veranda, laughing and chatting as they waited for the musicians to finish tuning up.

Breath coming short with anticipation, she hastened up the veranda steps. Her heart fell a little as she peered through the French windows. It was immediately apparent that *he*—she still couldn't bring herself to think of him by that frankly ridiculous title—hadn't arrived yet. A man of his dimensions couldn't hide in even the thickest crowd, and the dance hall was still mostly empty.

"Looking for someone, ma'am?"

She jumped. Breck had managed to sneak up without her notice, soft-footed as a cat. The waiter had a silver tray of champagne flutes, and a rather wicked gleam in his eye.

"Is *everyone* in on this?" Martha said in exasperation. "You all need some more excitement in your lives if you find other people's business this fascinating."

"Here at Shifting Sands, we pride ourselves in taking a keen personal interest in the happiness of our guests," Breck said, not looking the slightest bit repentant. He offered her the tray. "Please, take two. And if you will allow me to make a suggestion...I can highly recommend the view at the far end of the veranda."

Martha glared at him, which had absolutely no effect on his exceedingly smug smile. "You people clearly watch too many telenovelas. All this fuss over nothing."

Nonetheless, she took two of the champagne flutes, heading back outside. She found herself going against the tide, as other guests were heading into the main hall in expectation of the start of the dance. She didn't recognize many of the faces; more people must have boated over from the mainland just for the evening. Martha's skin prickled with the electric, feral energy of so many shifters gathered in one space.

Careful not to spill the drinks, she edged her way through the crowd, emerging back onto the veranda. The soft evening breeze should have been like a glass of cool water after the heady, pheromone-filled air inside…but the singing in her blood didn't diminish one whit. Instead, the fizzing excitement in her veins only grew, sparkling like the champagne.

Settle down, you fool dog, she told her coyote firmly as she followed the curving veranda. Honestly, it was ridiculous. No man justified this much panting anticipation, not even-

Then she rounded the corner of the building, and saw him.

She damn near dropped the champagne glasses. He was standing half-turned, his face in profile to her as he looked out to sea. The light of the full moon highlighted the stark, rugged planes of his features, and touched his iron-gray hair with pure silver. It gleamed from the vambraces encasing his powerful forearms, and from the massive, intricately-wrought steel plates protecting his shoulders.

He was, quite literally, a knight in shining armor.

Or no, not a knight—something more primal, more powerful. He looked like some hero out of ancient sagas, a demigod of war. If she hadn't known he was a flesh-and-blood man, she would have thought him made of marble and iron; a guardian statue, eternally ready to defend the island from any evil.

He'd told her he'd once been a king. Now, she believed it.

He turned his head, and his vast chest hitched as if he too had momentarily forgotten how to breathe. She shivered as his hungry gray eyes swept over her, slowly, from head to toe and back again.

"Thank you." His rasping voice was even hoarser than usual, just a scrape of stone on stone.

It took her two attempts to unstick her own tongue from the roof of her mouth. "For what?"

He made the slightest gesture at her own body. "For this memory."

He was impressed by *her* appearance? Martha stepped closer, drawn like a moth to a flame. She could scarcely believe that he was real. Only the fact that she still had both hands full stopped her from reaching out to touch him.

Although his armor covered his forearms and shoulders, only wide leather straps crossed his chest. His bare torso gleamed underneath, pale as marble in the moonlight. Where the straps met, over his heart, was a broad disc of silver, set with a single huge pearl clutched in the talons of an engraved sea dragon.

A belt worked with an intricate design of inlaid silver waves circled his waist. Form-fitting black leather pants clung to the hard curves of his thighs…and to other hard parts as well. Martha tore her eyes back upward, heat rushing into her face.

"Wh-what-" She swallowed, and tried again. "What on *earth* are you wearing?"

One corner of his mouth lifted fractionally, the closest he ever seemed to get to a smile. "Nothing on earth. This is what I wear under the sea, on formal occasions."

She blinked at him. "Well, life under the sea sure must be different to up here, is all I can say."

"Yes." There was a certain wry glint in his eye as he gestured at a couple of empty loops hanging from his belt. "Under the sea, I would go armed."

Holy Mother of God. Martha had a sudden vision of him with a sword in his hand, sweat-stained and savage, and felt weak at the knees.

His shadow of a smile dropped away as he misinterpreted her stunned silence. "I am sorry. I have no other formalwear. If you no longer wish me to accompany you-"

"No! I mean yes! Uh, that is, I definitely still want you. That. The dance. Um." Keeping hold of a train of thought was proving somewhat difficult. Martha struggled to pull herself back together, even though all she really wanted to do was stare at him. And then lick him. All over.

She cleared her throat, certain her own face must be flaming red. "Here," she said, thrusting a champagne glass at him to cover her own confusion. "Let's make a toast."

He hesitated, eying the glass without reaching for it. "I thought that was something to do with bread."

Her own mouth quirked. "Same word, different meaning. A toast is having a drink in honor of something."

"Ah." Very carefully, he took the glass from her. "And what shall we honor?"

Martha held her champagne up to him, and the moon. "To… memories. Old and new."

"To memories," he echoed softly.

Closing her eyes, Martha drank. The champagne tasted like moonlight, spreading silver through her veins.

To memories. The last time she'd drunk champagne as fine as this, it had been at her wedding. She remembered her husband's shining eyes as he'd made his vows to her. The vows he'd never, ever broken.

Oh, Manuel, Manuel. You were always faithful to me. Help me to be strong now.

A splutter interrupted her fervent prayer. Opening her eyes, she discovered the Master Shark was clearly struggling to contain a coughing fit. He was usually so dignified, she couldn't help but break into giggles.

"Oh, my," she said, wiping her eyes. "You aren't supposed to *chug* it. Don't you have champagne under the sea?"

"No." He put his now-empty glass down, still glaring at it with such mortal offense that it was a wonder it didn't melt into slag on the spot. "A fact for which I am now very grateful. Is all alcohol so…bubbly?"

"Only the good stuff." Unable to contain her curiosity any longer, she tapped a finger against one of the curving metal plates covering his forearm. It was, unmistakably, honest-to-God armor. "This must weigh a ton. Can you really dance in this stuff?"

The gleam was back in his storm-cloud eyes again, though this time it was a distinctly predatory look. Without a word, he held out his hand.

Setting aside her own champagne, she placed her hand in his. Her own looked very small, delicate as an autumn leaf against his hard, scarred palm. A thrill shot through every inch of her body as his powerful fingers closed, ever so gently, over hers.

"Come," he said, pulling her toward the dance hall. "I will show you."

CHAPTER 8

He could feel his mate's pulse thudding through her fingertips as he led her into the dance hall. Despite the excitement and arousal in her scent, there was an edge of apprehension as well.

He suspected he knew the cause. He attracted attention at the best of times. Here, dressed as he was, he stood out even more painfully. He'd worn his formal armor to honor her, but now he wondered if he'd made a mistake. He was used to drawing every eye, but he doubted Martha was.

When he ducked through the door, it was even worse than he'd feared. One musician accidentally inhaled through his instrument, producing a loud, discordant bleat. Most of the couples on the dance floor missed steps, doing double-takes up at him.

His shoulders tensed under his armor. If anyone dared to make his mate feel uncomfortable…

"Don't you dare," Martha snapped, bristling at a woman who'd started to raise a cellphone. "Have you no shame? How would you like it if I took *your* picture and stuck it up online for everyone to leer at?"

The young woman dropped her phone with a guilty expression. Martha tucked her hand more firmly into the crook of his arm, squeezing his rigid muscles. Holding her head high, she steered him onto the dance floor, ignoring the stares with the icy dignity of a born queen.

"Some people," she muttered, glaring at the nearest couple until they looked away sheepishly. "Honestly. Gawping at a man like he's an animal in a zoo." Her fingers tightened, as if in reassurance. "Just ignore those idiots. Don't let their bad manners spoil your evening."

She was concerned for *him*. Scarcely five feet tall, dressed in nothing more than thin silk over her soft curves, and yet she bared her teeth in his defense.

She caught his eye, and cocked her head. "What? Why're you looking at me like that?"

He wanted to carry her off and claim her. He wanted to hold her in his arms and never, ever let go. He wanted to fight with her, back to back, the two of them against the whole world.

But all he could do was lift her hand to his lips. Her breath hitched as he brushed her knuckles with the lightest of kisses. He closed his eyes, trying to memorize the precise scent of her skin.

When he opened his eyes again, hers had gone wide and dark. "What was that for?" she asked, breathless.

"You," he replied, lowering her hand again. He slid his other hand around her waist, as Breck had taught him. "Dance with me."

He was too tall for her to rest her left hand on his shoulder as the other couples were doing. Instead, she placed it in the crook of his arm, her warm fingers sliding under the cold plates of his armor. He could sense a hesitation in her touch. She was still unsure whether she could trust him.

He wished he had the words to reassure her. But he was a shark. He was not made for speech. He was made for silence, and darkness, and the hunt.

And to *move*.

She gasped as he swung her into the music. He could sense his prey's heartbeat from fifty miles away; following the loud, simple pulse of the drums was child's play in comparison. He let the rhythm sway him as easily as the ocean's currents.

Martha laughed out loud as he spun her round, her astonished eyes shining with delight. He read her desires in the brush of her fingertips on his and the sway of her hips, guiding her in return with the barest touch on her waist or the slightest press on her shoulder. She responded to his wordless suggestions so eagerly, it was as if they were linked mind-to-mind rather than hand-in-hand.

There was no breath for talking, thankfully. He could let his body say what his voice never could. She was the center of every circle, the focus of his every movement. No matter how she turned or twirled away, she always returned to him.

And always, he was there ready to catch her.

She was bright as the sun, alight with laughter and joy. He was a creature of cold water and colder blood, but every brush of her skin against his filled him with fire. He wanted more. He wanted to bury himself in her heat until she warmed him to the marrow of his bones. He wanted to bask in her warmth forever.

But he only had one night. These fleeting touches were all he would ever have, could ever have.

It will be enough. I promised that I would be content, if she would only give me one memory. I cannot ask for more.

He tried to stay in the moment, a shark's eternal now. He had to memorize every touch, every glance. He had to hoard enough of her heat to keep him warm for the rest of his life.

It will have to be enough.

But he knew it wouldn't.

CHAPTER 9

Good *Lord*, the man could dance.

Nigh on seven feet tall, broad as a barn and dressed in honest-to-God *armor*, and yet he put every other man there to shame. He moved as fluidly as water, every muscle under perfect control. No flourishes or fuss; every step, every turn had the smooth, economical grace of a hunting predator. He barely touched her, and yet led so effortlessly that Martha's feet seemed to follow of their own accord.

Dancing with him was as simple as breathing. It was life, it was light, it was pure joy. With her hands in his, she felt like she could dance the rest of her days.

It felt so right, it took her most of the evening to realize that something was badly wrong.

"Having a good time, ma'am?" Tex the bartender asked when she went to fetch more drinks.

"Oh my word, yes." Martha tucked her escaping flower back behind her ear, beaming at him. "I feel sixteen again. Though I bet my poor feet are going to be feeling every day their real age, come the morning."

Tex grinned back as he poured her a glass of ice water. "And, ah, is *he* enjoying himself, if you don't mind me asking? Kind of hard to tell, if you know what I mean."

Despite the lively salsa music, a twist of unease stabbed her stomach. She *did* know what Tex meant. No matter how beautifully the Master Shark's body moved to the rhythm, no hint of warmth showed in his face. She'd known rocks with more expression.

Is he enjoying himself? she wondered with a twinge of guilt. *Or am I just tormenting the poor man?*

She cast a glance back where she'd left him lurking in a shadowed corner—and caught a glimpse of his hulking, armored form ducking out the doorway. Her sense of unease grew.

He's probably just gone out to get some air, she tried to tell herself. *He's wearing inch-thick steel, for crying out loud. No doubt he needs to cool down. He'll be back.*

Nonetheless, her inner coyote nipped at her heels. Gathering up a glass of water, she hurried after him.

"Uh, Master Shark?" she called out self-consciously—for Heaven's sake, why couldn't the man have a proper name? "Everything all right?"

"Yes." He'd retreated to the end of the veranda again, both hands braced on the wooden railing, his back to her.

"I brought you some water." A little tentatively, she set it down on the rail, next to his left hand.

He didn't look round. "Thank you."

Almost, her nerve broke. But damn it, she was an alpha coyote. She'd faced down rattlesnake gangs and poachers, screaming toddlers and sullen teenagers. She'd never backed down from a challenge. She wasn't going to let a mere giant, brooding, armored shark king intimidate her now.

"Hey." She tugged on his arm, forcing him to look down at her. "Are you having a good time?"

"It is the best night of my life." Though his flat, toneless voice made it difficult to tell, she was pretty certain he sincerely meant it.

"Then what's wrong?"

Even as she said it, she knew exactly what was wrong. She knew what it was that kept his face still and expressionless. Much as she tried to deny it, she had the same cold, rock-like lump in her own chest.

Light flashed from his armor as his massive shoulders rose and fell in a long sigh. "I am sorry. I did not want to taint your enjoyment of this night."

Because we only *have this night.*

"I'm the one who should be apologizing to you." She looked down at her wedding ring, twisting it on her finger. "I wish-"

The words stuck in her throat. She couldn't lie to him. She couldn't wish that things had been different, that she'd never married Manuel. She couldn't regret her life with her husband, or her children, or her grand-children.

She jumped at his touch. Interlacing his fingers through hers, he turned her hand so that her wedding band caught the moonlight.

"The past makes us who we are," he said, his voice roughening with fierce intensity. "And I would not change anything about you. Not one thing."

Oh, this man.

This man who looked like a demon and danced like an angel. This man who sounded like he never spoke and said exactly what she needed to hear. This man could steal her heart.

And she knew that he already had.

She couldn't blame it on hormones, or her inner coyote. She could no longer deny that she'd fallen for him: hook, line and sinker. In her soul, she'd already broken her marriage vows.

Guilt and confusion roiled in her stomach. Tearing her gaze away from him, she found herself staring at the two champagne flutes they'd left here earlier. *To memories,* she'd proposed.

A cool breeze ruffled her hair, lifting it away from the nape of her neck. Manuel had always loved to kiss her there. The soft touch on her skin, the drifting sound of salsa music, the scent of jasmine—all combined into a sudden powerful, overwhelming memory:

"Go on," he whispered, his breath soft on her skin. *"You know you want to."*

The music thrilled through her bones, beckoning her forward. Nonetheless, she hesitated, pressing back against his warm, solid chest.

"I can't just leave you here by yourself," she protested. "What sort of wife would that make me?"

"What sort of a husband would I be if I demanded you stay chained to my side?" He kissed the nape of her neck again. "I want you to be happy, love. Even when I can't be the cause. Go. Go and dance."

Another dance, another time, so long ago she'd forgotten it until now.

The breeze whispered along her neck, soft as the kiss of a ghost.

I want you to be happy, love. Even when I can't be the cause.

The Master Shark had started to pull back, his face closing down again into an emotionless wall. She gripped his fingers tight, stopping him.

"What's your name?" she asked.

Surprise flashed across those iron-hard eyes. "My name?"

"Well, I'm pretty sure your mother didn't call you 'Master Shark.'" Despite her attempted lightness, her voice trembled. "And maybe I'm just old-fashioned, but I think I should know a man's name before I kiss him."

He looked like she'd walloped him across the back of the head with a baseball bat. "Before you...what?"

Stepping closer to him, she rested one hand on his chest. She could feel the wild thudding of his heart, perfectly in time with her own.

"Tell me your name," she said again.

He was silent for a moment longer, his eyebrows drawing down as if it had been so long since anyone had asked him this question, he was genuinely struggling to remember the answer.

"Finn," he said at last, softly. "My mother called me Finn."

Despite her racing pulse, she nearly choked on a snort of laughter. "*Finn?* Really?"

That shy, sweet, almost-smile flickered briefly across his face. "She had a terrible sense of humor."

"Finn," Martha repeated, smiling back. "It suits you. Well, Finn. I'm Martha."

"Yes," he whispered, all hungry intensity again. He bent down a little, locked on her as if nothing else existed in the whole world.

She darted her tongue over her lips. "And...I'm your mate."

He was so close now, she could see herself reflected in the dark pools of his eyes. Nonetheless he hesitated, his mouth barely a breath away from hers.

"Martha." The words sounded like they were being torn from his throat. "Do you truly want me?"

In answer, she closed the gap between them. The first touch of his lips on hers washed away any lingering doubts, filling her with certainty. This was *right*. With every part of her, body and mind and soul, she knew it.

He was her mate, and she was his. They were meant to be together. She wouldn't deny it any longer.

His taut muscles were hard as iron under her palm, yet his lips were gentle on hers. The unexpected softness of the kiss made her close her eyes, surrendering to the sweetness singing through her soul.

Oh, this man, this man.

My man.

She wanted to taste him, but he pulled away as she tried to deepen the kiss. Opening her eyes, she started to ask him what was wrong, but he stopped her question with a finger across her lips. His expression was rigidly controlled, but she could feel the urgency of his desire where she pressed against his body.

"No more," he growled, and her blood leaped at the barely-restrained feral edge to his voice. "Not here. But if you are sure..."

Too breathless for words, she nodded.

He didn't need to be invited twice. She gasped as he swept her up, lifting her as if she weighed nothing at all. Holding her in one arm, he vaulted over the veranda, so smoothly that she didn't even feel a bump. The instant his feet hit the ground, he was striding away, carrying her in the direction of the guest houses.

"No, wait," she managed to gasp out, as she realized he was headed for her cottage. "Let's go to yours."

He shook his head with a quick, sharp motion, never breaking stride. "Yours is closer."

"But-"

It was too late. He was already shouldering open the door, ducking his head to avoid hitting it on the lintel. Martha squirmed with embarrassment, hiding her face against his shoulder.

Oh, I should have cleaned up, I should at least have picked up my underwear-!

A strange, dry sound rattled deep in the Master Shark's—no, in *Finn's* chest. It took her a second to realize that he was laughing.

"I hope," he murmured in her ear, "that this means you were expecting me."

She risked a peek. There was no sign of the earlier chaos. Her clothes and scattered toiletries had been whisked out of sight, as if by magic. The rustic floorboards gleamed in the soft, romantic light of a few scattered candles, safely contained within tall glass jars. A fresh flower arrangement of jasmine and amaryllis perfumed the air. The bed had been made up with crisp white linens, and someone had scattered handfuls of rose petals across it.

"That Magnolia." Martha shook her head, half-touched, half-exasperated. "I *told* her not to bother the staff."

Finn made that hoarse, almost silent laugh again. His mouth was still set in its usual harsh line, but his eyes gleamed. "I am glad that she did."

Martha had to admit to herself, she was too. Still, the unmistakably bridal appearance of the bedroom made her feel suddenly shy. It had been so long since she'd been with a man, and she was no spring chicken. What if she disappointed him?

"Martha." There was an odd catch to Finn's voice, a slight note of hesitancy that she'd never heard before. The amusement had faded from his face. "I am a shark."

"Yes?" She blinked at him, confused. "So?"

He took a deep breath, tilting his head to indicate the gentle, romantic setting. "This is not…not in my nature. But if you desire softness…I will try."

Her own fears fled in the face of the raw vulnerability in his eyes. She slid down out of his arms, pressing herself fiercely against his body.

"I desire *you*," she said. Deliberately, she dug her nails into his muscled back. "Just as you are."

He made a low, wordless sound. His rough hands seized her hips, pulling her deliciously against his hard length. She let out a gasp as he crushed her back against the wall, her own desire surging at being surrounded by his intoxicating strength.

She tried to tug his head down so that she could kiss him, but he shook his head a little, pulling out of reach. For whatever reason, it was clear his mouth was out of bounds. She had to settle for nipping at his chest, near-drunk on the scent of him, the salt-sweat taste of his skin.

His powerful hands jerked her dress off her body with a sharp rip, his rough palms sliding over her skin as if he would lay claim to every inch. She practically whined in encouragement, thrusting herself shamelessly at him as she fought to undo his belt.

She managed to free him the same instant that his fingers slid under her panties. Oh *Lord,* he felt good in her hand, velvet-soft and iron-hard all at the same time, as much a contradiction as he himself was. The slickness already beading at his tip brought an answering gush between her own thighs.

"Oh yes," she gasped, as he slid a finger into her welcoming depths. She shuddered around him, squeezing his shaft hard in her fist. "Finn, I can't wait, now, please!"

Without a word, he tore her panties off. He lifted her effortlessly, her back against the wall, just as she'd secretly longed for. Martha wrapped her legs around him, and oh, oh, it was better than she could ever have imagined. She writhed in exquisite anticipation as his length slid through her folds—not entering yet, just testing her readiness.

She threw back her head as he rubbed against her just right, unable to hold herself back any longer. She cried out his name, scratching at his back as ecstasy exploded through her.

Though she couldn't have been more ready, she still caught her breath as his hardness pushed at her entrance. He was *big*, just as big as the rest of him. His shoulder muscles shook under her hands as he fought to go slowly.

But, oh, she didn't want slow. She wanted *him*.

Deliberately, she sank her teeth into his rigid neck. He jerked, and yes, at last, at *last* he lost his control. She was swept away as he slammed into her, finally giving her all of him, without holding back.

"Finn!" she cried out, overwhelmed with sensation, blind to everything but him. "Finn!"

He buried his face in the junction of her neck and shoulder as he strained into her. He didn't bite, but she felt the sharp press of clenched, jagged teeth against her skin. It was enough to send her tumbling over the edge again, washed away by pleasure.

It took a while to come back to herself. If he hadn't still been holding her up, she would have been a boneless heap on the floor. She leaned her forehead on his shoulder, safe and secure in his supportive arms, totally undone.

He held her until they were both breathing more steadily again. Then, with infinite care, he carried her over to the bed, laying her down on the soft sheets. Tired and tingling from head to toe, she stretched, watching as he stripped off his armor.

"I didn't warn you that *I'm* not gentle," she murmured, feeling a twinge of guilt. His white back was marked by livid stripes where she'd scratched him up. "You should have worn more armor."

His deep, rasping laugh rumbled through his chest as he curled up behind her. He kissed her shoulder softly, without a hint of teeth. "You bite like a shark."

Martha entwined her fingers through his, feeling utterly content. "But you don't bite."

He went still. "No. Not yet."

"Not yet?"

"It is how sharks mate."

Oh. He clearly meant *mate* mate; the permanent union of minds and souls, not just bodies.

Her inner coyote wagged its tail in eagerness, and Martha's own heart skipped a beat at the thought. To be fully joined to him, to know him inside and out, to see the secret soul behind the blank wall he presented to the world...oh, she wanted that.

But did he?

If he did...coyotes were pack animals. Any prospective mate had to be presented to the pack, and win their approval. And no matter how she tried, she couldn't imagine a Master Shark petitioning to join a bunch of dusty desert dogs. He and her pack just didn't fit in the same mental picture.

Maybe it was just as well he hadn't bitten her.

As if he'd sensed the darkening turn of her thoughts, his arm tightened around her. He drew the sheet up, covering them both. "Sleep now."

She nodded, pushing her worries down again. No sense fretting over the future. She nestled back into the warmth of his embrace, trying to recapture that glow of contentment.

"Finn?" she murmured, as exhaustion lowered her eyelids. "Did you *want* to bite me?"

He brushed her shoulder with his lips again...but if he answered, she was asleep before she heard it.

CHAPTER 10

He waited until he was certain she was asleep. It was difficult to pull himself away from her warm, relaxed body, but he wanted *all* her nights, not just this one.

Which meant that he had a difficult conversation ahead of him.

No one could move as silently as a shark. She never stirred as he collected his armor and slipped out the door.

The moon was dipping toward the horizon. He frowned at it as he dressed, calculating time zones. It would be very early in the morning in Atlantis, but it was his best chance of being able to make his petition in private.

Making sure his medallion of office was correctly placed over his heart, he headed for the sea. The tide was in, gentle waves lapping high up the white sands.

He let out his breath at the first welcome touch of salt water on his bare feet. It had been several days now since he had last shifted; his very bones felt dry. But there was no time to swim now. He needed his human voice for this.

Wading out to waist-depth, he touched the pearl set into his medallion. "My Empress."

The pearl glowed softly under his hand, letting him know that his call had been heard. Nonetheless, it took several minutes before the rippling waves around him flattened into mirror-like stillness.

"Master Shark?" The Pearl Empress's reflection peered up at him from the water. She appeared to be wearing nothing more than a sheet, so he guessed that she was using the scrying-pool in the royal apartment. "What is it? What's wrong?"

"Nothing. But I must ask a favor."

She pushed her tangled hair back from her face, her blue eyes concerned. "If you're calling at the crack of dawn, it must be more than 'nothing.' What sort of favor?"

"I seek your permission to bring a…guest with me, when I return to Atlantis."

"A guest?" Her eyebrows shot up. "You mean a dry-lander?"

Silently, he nodded. Behind his back, his fist clenched. *If she says no…*

She blew out her breath, looking annoyed, and his heart seized. "Master Shark, you are meant to be on *vacation*. Not negotiating diplomatic alliances."

"Not a diplomatic guest. A personal one."

She blinked. "Master Shark, you are making no sense whatsoever."

"My Empress." He took a deep breath, setting his shoulders. "I would like permission to bring my mate to Atlantis."

She stared at him.

"Please," he added, voice cracking on the unaccustomed word.

"He wants to do *what?*" The Royal Consort, who clearly must have been listening in, appeared over the Empress's shoulder. The indigo-haired sea dragon was bare-chested and sleep-tousled, but still had his sword in his hand.

His stomach sank at their looks of shock. "I understand that it is unprecedented to bring a land-shifter to Atlantis. But, my Empress, if I have served you-"

"Master Shark, you can bring anyone you like here," the Empress interrupted. Despite her words, she still looked stunned. "I owe you more than I can ever repay, after all. But…you really met your mate? On land?"

"She is a coyote shifter, a pack leader and matriarch of great standing," he said, wishing that his harsh voice was capable of showing the pride he felt. "Her name is Martha Hernandez."

"Martha," the Empress repeated, a brilliant smile breaking across her face. "Oh, I can't wait to meet her. Of course you must bring her to Atlantis."

The Royal Consort did not seem to share his mate's evident pleasure in the news. The sea dragon was still studying him, his stern features impossible to read.

He had feared that the Royal Consort might prove to be his enemy in this. There was no love lost between them—they both carried scars from the other's teeth, though they had since made an uneasy peace with each other. And the sea dragon was a Knight-Poet of the First Water, honor-bound and oath-sworn. Although the Royal Consort was a little more flexible than most, sea dragon Knights were still rigid adherents to custom.

He will seek to deny me. He will argue that it is too dangerous to allow a land-shifter into Atlantis, that it would put the Empress at risk.

When the Royal Consort spoke, though, his words were utterly unexpected. "Master Shark...does she wish to come?"

He hesitated for a moment, caught off-guard. "We have not yet discussed it. But we are mates. We must be together."

The Royal Consort nodded fractionally, as if he'd been expecting this answer. He touched the Empress's shoulder.

"My heart," he said softly. "May I speak with the Master Shark alone for a moment?"

The Empress narrowed her eyes at him. "John, don't you even think about objecting based on some silly tradition. We have sea shifters venturing onto land now. It's only right that we should welcome other shifters here in return."

He shook his head, the golden charms braided into his hair catching the light. "I have no objection to that. But nonetheless there are security concerns that I must discuss with him, warrior to warrior. I am Imperial Champion as well as your Consort. It is a matter of duty."

The Empress gave him an unconvinced look, but gave way. "I look forward to meeting your mate, Master Shark. I'll be in contact to sort out the practicalities."

The Royal Consort waited a few moments, until she had left the room. "Master Shark," he said, his tone hardening, "if your mate does not want to come to Atlantis, will you stay with her on land?"

The question hit him like a blow. He had been so focused on pursuing his mate, he had not given much thought to what he would do if he caught her.

What if Martha *didn't* wish to come to Atlantis?

"That," he said coldly, not letting any hint of the sudden doubt he felt show in his expression, "is not a matter for your concern."

"With respect, Master Shark, it *is*." The sea dragon didn't flinch at all from his glare. "I am responsible for the Empress's well-being. And she needs you. The Pearl Empire needs you."

He could not deny the truth of the Royal Consort's words. The Pearl Empress had only reclaimed her throne recently. There were still too many enemies circling round her, hunting any opportunity to tear her down.

And he had sworn an oath to her father that he would protect her with his life.

"I am sorry," the Royal Consort said softly, when he didn't speak. "I know full well what it is to be caught between duty and love. And in truth, I cannot tell you to pick duty over your mate. *I* tried to do that, and I know now that it would have destroyed me utterly, had I succeeded."

It was even harder than usual to force words out of his tight throat. "Then what would you have me do?"

"You must persuade your mate to come to Atlantis. For the sake of *my* mate." The Royal Consort met his eyes levelly. "For all our sakes."

CHAPTER 11

Martha jerked awake to an unholy shrieking rattling her eardrums.

"Mother of God!" Only the tangled sheets stopped her from falling out of bed. She thrashed to free herself, heart pounding. "Is there a fire?"

Finn was already awake, sitting up in bed with his back against the wall. Silently, he pointed at her vibrating cellphone.

"Oh." Sitting up herself, Martha caught the device before it walked itself off the dresser. She cleared her throat, rubbing at her sticky eyes. "Hello?"

"Ma!" Martha's heart leaped at the panic in Nita's voice. "Are you sick? What's wrong? Do you need to come home?"

Finn cocked his head, clearly about to ask a question. Martha slapped a hand across his mouth before he could speak, worried that Nita would overhear him.

"Nothing's wrong," Martha said into the phone. "What's the matter? Why are you calling?"

"Because you haven't called us for a whole day! We thought something must have happened to you!"

"Oh." Martha glanced guiltily at Finn. "Sorry, honey. I was, um, busy."

She felt his lips twitch in amusement against her palm. She pressed down harder, mouthing: *Keep quiet, you.*

"Ma," Nita said, sounding suspicious. "You're always busy, and it's never stopped you from finding time to check up on everyone. You call us six times a day, and then suddenly nothing? What's going on?"

"Nothing!" Martha yelped, trying not to look at the naked seven-foot hunk of muscle next to her. "Nothing's going on. Just enjoying a nice peaceful vacation, like you wanted."

"Oh." Nita fell silent for a moment. "Guess I should be careful what I wish for. I was worried about you, Ma."

"Is that abuela?" Ximena yelled in the background. "Manny! Manny! Abuela isn't dead after all!"

"Abuela!" Manny sounded about to burst into tears. "Come back from Heaven! I miss you!"

"Uh, the kids may have been a little worried too," Nita said, over the howls and sobbing promises to be good if she'd just come home.

It took fifteen minutes for Martha to reassure five-year-old Manny that she hadn't *actually* become an angel, and that furthermore she was absolutely, definitely coming home at the end of the week. Then of course Ximena needed to talk to her abuela for just as long as Manny had, and then Nita's wife Xo had a question about the upcoming church bake sale, and then Martha needed to talk to Nita again about Roddie, because if he didn't stop provoking the rattlesnakes someone was going to get bit, and oh, while we're talking...

By the time Martha finally managed to hang up, her voice was as hoarse as Finn's. She sighed as she dropped the phone back onto the dresser.

"Sorry," she said to him, taking her hand off his mouth at last. "Didn't want them to hear you."

He nodded, but his face had gone back to that rock-like impassiveness he'd had when they'd first met. Throughout the long call, she'd had a strange sense of him retreating further into himself.

She issued a smile at him, hoping to spark one in return. "It's just that we'd have lost the whole day to answering fool questions if they'd realized what was up. You know how families are."

He looked down, rolling something between his palms. "No. I do not."

She kicked herself for walking straight into that one. Whatever shark families were like, she doubted they were as nosy—not to mention noisy—as a coyote pack. Especially her own brood.

"What've you got there?" she asked, desperate to change the subject.

He folded his fingers, hiding whatever it was in his vast fist. "You asked me something last night."

She blinked at him, thrown. "I did?"

"Whether I wanted to bite you." He still didn't look at her.

"Oh." Her heart thumped against her ribs.

He didn't know what my pack was like, what he was letting himself in for. Now he does.

She swallowed. "Well...do you?"

He turned his head at last, and the intensity of his gray eyes took her breath away. "Yes. I want to be your mate. Fully."

Holy Mother of God, did he have a *wedding ring* in his hand? Martha couldn't even begin to imagine why he would be carrying one around, but it was the only thing she could think of to explain the look on his face.

"Yes," she said, blinking back sudden, strange tears. "I want that too."

His knuckles whitened. "But I am what I am. I am the Master Shark, and the Voice of the Pearl Empress. No matter how I might wish it otherwise, I have responsibilities that cannot be set aside."

Her heart plummeted right down to the socks she wasn't wearing. Of course he wasn't free to leave the sea. He'd given her his true name, but he was still the Master Shark. Doubtless he had responsibilities she couldn't even imagine.

He looked back down at his closed fist. "I had thought to ask you to join me in Atlantis," he said, very quietly.

"What? Me?" She stared at him in disbelief. "I'm a coyote, not a fish!"

"The Pearl Empress has personally granted permission for you to come, and there are ways for dry-landers to live under the sea. If you wanted."

Oh, she wanted. She wanted *him*. But enough to give up her whole life? Everything she knew? Her family?

"Finn." She put her hand on the side of his face, making him meet her eyes again. No matter what, they had to be honest with each other. "I want to be with you. More than anything. But you heard my family. They fall apart when I don't call for a day, what do you think would happen if I announced I was taking off to live under the sea? Do you even have cellphones in Atlantis?"

He shook his head, the barest motion.

"So what do we do?" Martha whispered.

His shoulders fell in a long sigh. He got up, reaching for his clothes. "I do not know."

She bit her lip, watching him dress. Even now, with her heart made of lead, the sight of his muscled body made heat surge through her veins.

"Could we...figure it out later?" she asked, tentatively. "No matter what happens, we have the rest of this week. Can we take a vacation from our real lives, just for a little while?"

He went still, his back to her. "Yes. We could do that."

She slipped out of bed herself, padding over to him. Wrapping her arms around his waist, she leaned her forehead against the hollow of his spine, breathing in his salt-sea scent.

Four days.

Four days before reality caught up with them. Four days to find a way that they could be together.

Otherwise four days would be all they had.

CHAPTER 12

She was not going to come with him.

His hopes had ebbed away like the tide as she'd chattered to her family, leaving his heart bleak and bare. Her dark eyes had been alight, emotions darting across her expressive face as brightly as shoals of tropical fish.

His kind were solitary by nature. Sharks might come together for a purpose—to feed, to mate, to defend territory—but it was usually a brief-lived alliance. In his arrogance, he had assumed that a pack was no more than an unusually persistent hunting group.

Now, having heard her talk to hers, he knew just how badly he'd been wrong. It was clear that a pack was more like a coral reef—a symbiotic relationship, lives so completely intertwined that they were like a single, unified being.

And he had asked her to leave that behind. Trade her busy, sun-lit, joyous existence for the dark silence of the deep.

She was not going to come with him.

And she had not wanted her pack to know that he even existed.

Martha glanced over her shoulder at him, her brow furrowed, and he made himself push his despair down into the abyss of his soul. He had promised her four days. A vacation from their real lives, she'd called it.

If these four days were all that they could ever have, he would not spoil them with his insatiable hunger for more.

"You all right?" she asked him. "Feet okay?"

"I am fine." In truth, his feet were aching abominably. But the pain was a welcome distraction from the deeper pain in his heart.

Martha turned, putting her hands on her hips and glaring up at him. "No heroics, Finn. You can't possibly be used to hiking."

"I spend a great deal of time in human form." He lengthened his stride to catch up with her, forcing himself not to limp. "I must, in order to be the Voice of the Empress. Different types of sea shifters cannot talk with each other in our native forms, so we gather in Atlantis in order to speak with human voices. I am accustomed to walking."

Unfortunately, this stony dirt trail was a far cry from the smooth, coral-paved streets of Atlantis. The resort guidebook had described this as a 'short, easy hike.' If that was true, then he dreaded to think what a dry-lander might consider a *difficult* trek.

Martha poked him in the center of his chest with one finger, still looking unconvinced. "Well, you just say if you want to take a break, okay? No shame in admitting you need a rest."

She trotted ahead again, her sneaker-clad feet flashing easily across the uneven terrain. She looked as fresh as she had two hours ago, when they'd first started off. Watching the glide of the muscles in her strong brown legs, he was strongly tempted to suggest they did indeed take a break...though not to rest.

She cast him another glance over her shoulder, but this time her eyes were mischievous rather than concerned. "I'm beginning to think you're lagging behind deliberately, you know."

"I am admiring the view." He let his gaze drift over her curves, enticingly displayed in cut-off shorts and a filmy top. "You said that was the purpose of a hike."

"Oh, you." Nonetheless, there was an extra sway to her hips as she turned away. "Come on, keep up. We must be nearly there."

He could hear the familiar murmur of the sea now, under the foreign trills and squawks of dry-land birds and insects. The scent of moisture in the air grew stronger as they followed the trail up the last few switchbacks.

"Oh my." Martha sighed in delight as they finally emerged out of the jungle and into the sunlight again. "Would you just look at that."

A glittering waterfall tumbled down the cliffs, casting sparkling rainbows over the worn rocks. Fifty feet below them, freshwater met the ocean in a spray of white foam. A tiny, perfect cove surrounded the waterfall, the lush emerald jungle spilling over onto the narrow strip of silver sand.

Martha's warm hand crept into his. They stood for a while in silence, just looking.

Land and sea, water and air. The stream needed the rock to turn its eternal movement into beauty; the shore would be bare as bone without the water. It all came together in perfect union.

He looked at Martha, and knew that he needed her as much as the land needed the water, the water the land.

I will not give her up. There must be a way.

"Would you shift for me?" he asked.

She glanced up at him in surprise, startled out of her rapt contemplation of the waterfall. "You want to see my animal? Here? Now?"

He lifted one shoulder in a small shrug. "I have never seen a coyote."

If he better understood her nature, perhaps he would see a way forward for them. He needed to know her secret soul if he had any chance of finding a way to bridge their two worlds.

Martha ducked her head, looking a little shy. "Well...okay then. But don't set your expectations too high. Coyotes aren't exactly majestic."

Stepping back into the shade of the tree line, she kicked off her sneakers. His blood surged as she pulled her top over her head. It was all he could do to stay still. His hands clenched at his sides, itching to reach for her lush breasts.

From the swift downward flick of her eyes and sudden smug

smile, she knew full well the effect she was having on him. She took rather longer than was strictly necessary about unfastening her bra, sliding the straps slowly down over her brown shoulders.

"You sure it's my coyote you want to see?" she teased him.

"Yes," he growled, hanging onto his self-control by his fingernails. "First."

She turned her back on him, casting a coy glance over her shoulder. Bending at the waist, she pulled her shorts and panties down over her soft thighs. Her round backside rolled seductively at him, her scent beckoning from her exposed pink cleft.

That he could not resist. Without conscious thought, he was behind her, pushing her down to her hands and knees. She let out a triumphant giggle that turned into a gasping moan as he slid his fingers through her inviting folds.

She was already wet for him, slick and eager. She ground against him as he pushed into her with two fingers, his other hand reaching round to find her hard nipples. He clenched his teeth, fighting the urge to sink them into her shoulder as she shuddered around him.

She whined, spreading her legs wider, backside thrusting into the air. "More, Finn. I need you."

He needed her, more than he could ever say. Shoving down his own garments, he mounted her, too blind with need to be gentle. Her hot depths welcomed him. She enfolded him like the sea itself, powerful and irresistible. The rhythm of her pulsing tides swept him helplessly to his own climax.

"Martha," he gasped, spilling himself into her, coming home. "My mate!"

He collapsed down against her, only just managing to catch himself on his hands and spare her his full weight. Breathing hard, he leaned his forehead against her shoulder. She let out a contented hum, arching back against him.

"I win," she said smugly.

He let himself smile, since she couldn't see his face. "I would still like to see your coyote."

She laughed, wriggling out from under him. "Well, since you asked so nicely…"

Pushing herself to her feet, she took a few steps away, holding eye contact. He drank in the sight of her naked, sweat-beaded skin, the soft curve of her belly, the beautiful lines that crinkled around her smiling eyes.

She shook herself, a whole-body shimmy. And in an instant, the woman was gone.

The breath sighed out of him. "Yes. That is who you are."

She had the same laughing amber eyes, the same proud tilt to her head. Her alert ears were made to catch every sound, her slim muzzle to follow the faintest scent. Her lush fur hid a thousand subtle shades of sand and rock. She would be swift and silent in the hunt, subtle and relentless.

Her long tongue lolled out in an unmistakable smile. She trotted over, nudging her nose under his hand. He tentatively stroked her head, astonished by the texture. He'd never touched a furred creature before. Soft, so soft, but all strength underneath. So warm.

She half-closed her eyes, leaning into his touch with evident pleasure. He ran his palm over her neck, exploring the thickness of her ruff, her hard, muscled shoulders. Her plumed tail thumped on the ground.

She was made for open skies and wide desert. For running all night, slender legs and strong feet devouring the miles. Oh, they were well matched indeed. Though their forms could not have been more different, they were both made for speed, and stamina, and the hunt.

And that made their situation even worse than he had thought.

He had feared that they were too different from each other. Instead, they were too alike. What would she do in the enclosed, underwater walls of Atlantis? She would be a shark in a tank, unable to express her true nature. Endlessly circling, endlessly yearning. Trapped.

One pointed ear cocked in his direction. She nipped at his wrist, not breaking the skin, but a clear press of teeth into his flesh.

Growling deep in her throat, she shook his arm, as if to drag him out of his spiraling thoughts.

"My mate." He pressed his face into her warm fur, breathing in her clean, dry scent. "You are beautiful."

Her eyes gleamed sidelong at him. Without warning, she sprang, knocking him backward with her front paws pinning his chest. Her broad wet tongue licked his face from chin to forehead.

He spluttered, laughing out loud in surprise. She froze, head cocked down at him, and he froze too.

He'd forgotten himself. He'd exposed his teeth.

She shimmered, and the warm fur turned into warm skin, pressed against his. Still straddling him, Martha gently touched his mouth.

"Show me again," she said.

His jaw tightened. "No."

She leaned down, pressing her mouth against his. He closed his eyes, unable to withstand her gentle insistence. Parting his lips, he allowed her soft, sweet tongue to explore the serrated points of his teeth.

He had a triple row of them, like all his kind. Shark teeth in a human mouth.

She pulled away again, with a last, lingering kiss. "I like your smile. You should do it more often."

"I do." He could not help the ironic curl of his mouth, though habit kept his teeth safely hidden this time. "When I wish to alarm people."

She brushed her thumb across his lower lip. "You don't alarm me. Finn, this isn't going to work if you keep trying to hide who you really are."

He dropped his head back with a sigh, staring up at the cloudless blue sky. "You have always seen me as I truly am. I do not want you to start seeing me as others do."

She folded her arms on his chest, leaning her chin on them. "Like people do in Atlantis?"

Silently, he nodded.

"If I join you there, then I'm going to find out, you know."

He lifted his head, staring at her. She met his eyes steadily, her own very serious.

Is she truly still considering it?

"I showed you my animal." Martha sat up, the movement swift and decisive. "I think it's time you showed me yours."

CHAPTER 13

Magnolia nudged Martha in the ribs with her elbow. "The water must be deep enough now," she whispered, casting a surreptitious glance at the back of the boat. "When's he going to shift?"

Martha folded her arms, scowling. "Probably never, since you folk have made such a production out of it."

Yesterday, she'd thought it would be simple. That they'd just walk on down to the sea, and he would show her. But apparently he couldn't shift close to the shore. Whatever sort of shark he was—and she *still* didn't know—required a lot of space.

Hence why they had joined today's whale-watching expedition. Or, since gossip seemed to spread like wildfire on this island, what was now unofficially a shark-watching expedition. Martha was pretty sure the boat wasn't usually *this* packed. Especially not with off-duty resort staff.

"I promise, I did not breathe a word to anyone." Magnolia held up one hand like a Boy Scout. "But the staff already knew who he was. You can't blame them for being curious."

Martha switched her glare to Tex and Breck, who were perched on the narrow benches opposite. The pair at least had the decency to look moderately guilty. Tex tipped his hat at her in a *sorry, ma'am* sort of way.

Martha sighed. As a coyote, she really couldn't take anyone to task for nosiness. She had to admit, she'd have done just the same, in their place.

"Well, I expect we're all going to be disappointed," she said grumpily. "He's no fool. He'll have worked out you all haven't developed a sudden fascination with dolphins."

Though if Finn *was* aware of the ulterior motives of half the party, he gave no sign of it. He stood at the very back of the boat, staring out at the churning waves with an expression even more impenetrable than usual.

"Okay, ladies and gentlemen," Travis called from the tiller. He steered the boat one-handed with the ease of long practice, his other shading his eyes as he scanned the horizon. "We're coming up to the area where the humpback whale pods are usually found, so keep your eyes peeled."

Well, that answers the question of who's genuinely here to see whales, Martha thought, as the half-dozen or so other resort guests eagerly craned their necks.

"Sorry," she muttered to Magnolia, feeling a little sheepish. "You were telling the truth about not gossiping. I shouldn't've snapped at you."

Magnolia patted her knee, smiling in understanding. "No apology necessary. Keep a lookout for those whales. They really are quite a sight."

"I see a fin!" one of the other resort guests called out excitedly, pointing. "Coming right at us! Is that a whale?"

Travis narrowed his eyes. "No, wrong shape. That looks like a…oh. Hm."

"A what?" Martha asked, when he didn't finish his sentence.

"That's definitely a tiger shark." As people jerked back from the sides of the boat, Travis hastily added, "Don't worry, they're perfectly harmless. We're lucky to see one, actually. They're very shy."

Martha glanced at the back of the boat, but Finn was still there.

His gaze followed the circling shark. He tilted his head a little, eyes going distant.

"There, see, it's gone," Travis said, as the fin slipped back under the water again. "Nothing to worry about."

Balancing herself against the rocking motion of the boat, Martha made her way back to Finn. "Did you do that?" she asked under her breath.

He shot her a wry, sideways glance. "Do you mean call her, or send her away?"

"Her?"

"She was a female. A proud grandmother, in fact, the matriarch of these waters."

"You could tell all that just on sight?"

He shook his head, returning his gray gaze to the dark waters. "She told me."

Martha could communicate somewhat with wild coyotes, but not like *that*. Then again, she wasn't the Master Coyote or any other such grand title.

"Uh, no, those aren't dolphins," Travis was saying. "Those would be, um, more sharks. Hammerheads, I think." He cleared his throat. "Ah, sir?"

The Master Shark glanced back at him.

Travis grimaced. "Are we likely to see *any* whales on this trip?"

"No." The Master Shark looked past him at the other guests, who stared back with confused expressions. "My apologies."

"Well, I for one am just fascinated by all these wonderful sharks!" Magnolia said brightly. "What's that fine fellow over there, Travis? He's a real beauty."

Travis followed her pointing finger, and made a slightly strangled noise. "That…that would be a Great White."

Magnolia didn't so much as bat an eyelash. "How lovely. Never seen one of those before."

The Great White shark swept under them, a sleek, silent shadow nearly as long as the boat. Martha leaned over the side, fascinated.

Despite its name, it wasn't actually white. Its upper side was a steely blue-gray, perfectly matching the water around it.

"It really is quite pretty," she said. "Though it's not as big as I expected, from the movies."

Beside her, Finn let out a short rasp of laughter. "You would like to see a bigger shark?"

"That wasn't a very subtle hint, was it?" Martha admitted. She met Finn's eyes, lifting her chin in challenge. "Well? You going to show me one?"

He surprised her with a brief, fierce kiss, his jagged teeth hard and hungry against her lips. Then, without a further word, he dove into the sea.

One of the guests shrieked, her hands flying to her mouth. "He fell in! He'll be eaten alive!"

"He'll be just fine, ma'am," Tex drawled. "He's—whoa!"

They all grabbed for the rail as the boat bucked like an ornery bull. Travis cursed, fighting the tiller against the sudden surge of the ocean. Martha's stomach flipped over as the boat bobbed and spun.

The waves settled down again, and so did the boat. Martha prised her fingers off the rail, breathing hard. Several of the guests had been flung clear out of their seats, although thankfully no one had fallen overboard.

"What was that?" Breck gasped, helping Magnolia back to her bench.

"I think that," Tex said, staring down into the ocean, "was *that*."

Martha looked over the side, and the breath froze in her throat.

Great White? she'd asked him once, and *No*, he'd replied.

The Great White shark sported around his vast form like a Chihuahua begging a Great Dane to play. The other sharks joined it, circling around the huge, rising shape in silent worship. That enormous maw could have snapped any of them up in a single mouthful, yet none of them showed any fear.

Why would they? Martha thought, dumbstruck with awe. *He's their Master.*

"Now *that* has to be a whale," one of the other guests commented, raising a camera.

"I'm...pretty sure it isn't." Travis's knuckles were white on the tiller. "Please don't take any pictures. They'd make headlines worldwide if they leaked out, and I doubt he'd appreciate being front-page news."

"Travis?" Even Magnolia had gone pale under her tan. "Exactly what kind of shark is that?"

"One that's been extinct for about five million years." He swallowed hard. "That's a megalodon. Biggest predator that's ever existed, land or sea."

The boat rocked again as that vast shape swept underneath them. He was eighty feet long if he was an inch, iron-gray from nose to tail. And oh, he was *beautiful*. She'd thought him overwhelming enough on land, but it was as nothing compared to the sight of him in his natural domain. He moved as fluidly as water, like the soul of the sea made flesh.

Several of the other guests screamed as his back broke the surface alongside the boat. They clutched each other in fear, staring up at the enormous fin rising higher than a yacht's sail.

"It's all right! It's all right!" Travis yelled, trying to calm the panic. "He's a guest. He won't hurt anyone."

Martha reached out, stretching to her limit. Her hands hungered to touch that powerful gray form, just as he'd buried his own hands in her fur.

"Uh, ma'am?" Travis cleared his throat. "I'm sorry, but could you please not do that? If he gets any closer, he's going to swamp the boat."

Finn must have heard him, because his huge bulk backed off a little. He rolled in the water, looking up at her through the waves. His deep black eye looked tiny in comparison to his enormous bulk, but it was still bigger than her entire head.

"I see you," she said softly, just for him. "I still see you."

That vast jaw worked. She was certain he was smiling.

Then he dove back into the depths, and was gone.

∽

He came back out of the sea at dusk, emerging from the waves like some ocean god. Martha was waiting for him on the beach, her legs comfortably propped up on a deckchair, a margarita in her hand.

"Hello, you," she said, smiling. "Have a good swim?"

He bent to kiss her. "You were not worried?"

She shook her head, curving her hand around his damp neck to pull him back down again. His lips tasted of salt and wildness, more intoxicating than any cocktail.

"I guessed you needed to spend some time out there," she said, when they broke apart at last. She passed him the towel she'd kept ready. "I get antsy if I don't shift every few days, so I thought it was probably the same for you."

He nodded, drying himself off. There was something looser, more relaxed about the set of his shoulders. When he sat down, he actually leaned back into his deckchair rather than sitting bolt-upright like a soldier on duty.

"I had not visited these waters for some time," he said. "The sharks needed to speak with me. Some trouble with illegal hunters, and pollution from a wreck…small matters in the grand scheme of the Pearl Empire, but important to my people nonetheless."

"There are shark shifters here?"

"A few. But mainly just sharks. They are mine, as much as the shifters are. And it is my responsibility to speak for those who have no voice."

Martha took his hand, interlacing her small fingers through his broad, rough ones. "Travis said you were a—I forget the word. Some kind of ancient shark."

"Megalodon."

"That was it. I didn't even know that you could get shifters from extinct species. Were your parents like you?"

"No." His eyes were fixed on the horizon. "A megalodon is only born in times of great change, as a sign that the sharks must unite behind a single ruler in order to survive. My mother was human, my father a bull shark. When they realized what I was, they gave me up to be raised by the Circle of Teeth—the five most powerful shark shifters in the sea, our leaders at the time—so that they could prepare me for my destiny."

"To be the Master Shark?"

"No." His mouth quirked. "To be the Pearl Emperor. Ruler of all the shifters of the sea."

She stared at him.

He made his dry, rasping laugh. "I was not very good at fulfilling my destiny."

"I'm glad of that," Martha said, faintly. "I don't think I'd've made a very good Empress."

His smile widened, and warmth flooded through her as she realized he was no longer trying to hide his jagged teeth. "I was once a king. But you will always be a queen."

"Oh, you." She leaned against him, his bare skin cool and damp against hers. She wasn't sure she should ask, but a coyote never could resist a story. "So what happened? With your destiny, I mean."

To her relief, his massive shoulder stayed loose and relaxed under her cheek. "The Circle believed that I was born to overthrow the sea dragons, and usher in the age of sharks. They trained me in war from the age of five. I embraced my role. I honed myself into a weapon with one purpose—to hunt down and kill the sea dragon Emperor. And one night, after years of battle with his defenders, I caught him. Alone and unguarded."

His gray eyes were distant, looking back across the decades. "And I found that he was just a young man, the same age as myself. Not a monstrous, all-powerful tyrant. Just a lonely, quiet man, raised from infancy to perform a particular role whether he liked it or not."

"Just like you." She squeezed his hand. "So you let him go?"

His chest vibrated with his wry chuckle. "No. I tried to kill him."

Martha blinked. "Okay. That was not where I was expecting this story to go."

"We fought, and the sea turned red around us. But I was so focused on the battle, I didn't realize that I too was being hunted. A human submarine. They could not see the Emperor, for mythic shifters can hide themselves from human sight, but they saw me all too well." He touched a pale, starburst-shaped scar that marked his side. "I had his throat in my teeth, a heartbeat away from delivering the kill bite, when their torpedoes hit me. And when I woke up, I was on a deserted island. And he was there too, swearing at me, his hands pressed to my side while his magic kept my life-blood in my veins."

Martha traced the radiating lines of the scar. It wrapped around him from backbone to belly button. She shivered at the thought of the torpedo exploding inside his body.

"Why did he save you?" she asked.

"He always claimed that it was so that he could kill me himself." His gray eyes were the color of spring rain, softer than she had ever seen before. "He was a sea dragon, with a sea dragon's honor. He said it would be shameful to take advantage of my wound. So for a month, he tended to me, alone and in secret. And by the time I had recovered enough to resume our battle…neither of us wanted to."

"Most problems can be solved by folks just sitting down and listening to each other." Martha nestled closer to him, running one finger up the line of his abs. "What did the other sharks say when you told them you weren't going to kill the Emperor?"

His muscles flexed under her touch, the rippling ridges hardening. Parts further south were hardening too. "If you persist in that, you will not hear the end of the story."

Martha giggled, her own heat rising at the feel of his cool skin. "Better make it quick then."

"There is not much more to tell. I did not tell my people what had transpired, because they would have turned on me as a traitor. Instead, I publicly challenged the Emperor for the Pearl Throne. If I won, he would step down; if he did, the sharks would swear fealty to his Empire. He accepted. We fought one-on-one, before the eyes of both the Sea Council and the Circle of Teeth. And this time he bested me, fairly and honorably."

Martha cocked an eyebrow at him. "Did you let him?"

His sharp teeth gleamed. He didn't say anything.

"Cunning as a coyote." She nipped his shoulder teasingly. "So you *were* born to lead the sharks to a new destiny. But it was to bring them into the Pearl Empire rather than overthrow it."

He nodded. "The Circle of Teeth was disbanded, and the Emperor named me the Master Shark. The first and only one of my kind to have a place on the Sea Council. I was...not loved for it. By either the sharks or the sea dragons."

Her heart went out to him. She couldn't even begin to imagine what it must be like, to be viewed as a failure—or even a traitor—by his own people. Or how hard it must be to have to work every day with age-old enemies who thought he was some kind of blood-thirsty monster. No wonder he was so closed and remote.

"But you had the Emperor on your side, at least?" she asked. "Your friend?"

"My oath-brother," he said softly. "For a time, yes." His hand captured hers, flattening it over his heart. "But that is a longer story, for another day."

She leaned on his shoulder, watching the sun sink into the sea, his heartbeat slow and steady under her palm. She thought over all he'd told her.

He can't ever leave the sea.

Some small, selfish part of her still wanted to ask him to come home with her, to join her pack. But her tiny family dramas paled in comparison to *his* huge, empire-spanning responsibilities. How could she ask him to walk away from his life's work? From who he *was*?

And beside which, he was a shark. There was nowhere for him to shift in the dry Arizona desert.

Nonetheless, she was certain that he would come, if she asked. He would burn himself to dry skin and bone for her sake, and never count the cost.

Love meant sacrifice. She knew that, down to the marrow of her bones.

She'd sacrificed romantic daydreams of finding her one true mate for the homely, everyday love of a good human man. She'd sacrificed sleep and time and sometimes her own sanity to raise her children. She'd shed blood and tears and sweat to protect her pack.

So many sacrifices in her life. And she'd never regretted any of them. Not a single one.

I won't regret this one either, she told herself.

Nonetheless, it took her a few minutes to work up the courage to do what she must. "Finn?"

He looked down at her, resurfacing from whatever depths of memory he'd been lost in.

"I want…" She licked her lips, throat dry. "I want to come with you to Atlantis."

CHAPTER 14

This is wrong.

Every one of his instincts screamed it at him as he watched Martha struggle into the wetsuit she'd borrowed from the resort. She was a desert creature, made for light and laughter. What was he doing taking her into the cold, silent depths?

But she'd been adamant that this was what she wanted.

"I want you as my mate," she'd said last night, her soft fingertips silencing his protests. "And I've seen both sides to you now—Finn, and the Master Shark. You can't rip yourself in two, pretending one half doesn't exist. And I wouldn't want you to. I can be happy anywhere, as long as I'm with you."

He feared that would not be true. But she was as single-minded as a shark on a blood trail. The best he'd been able to do was to convince her to let him take her on a short visit to Atlantis. Today, he would show her what her life would truly be like if she joined him under the waves.

Then they would return to Shifting Sands. And she would make her final decision.

"Stop looking like your dog died," Martha said, zipping up the wetsuit. "Or your goldfish, or whatever it is you people keep as pets. Do you have pets in Atlantis?"

"No. Martha, you don't yet understand how different-"

"Nope, and I don't intend to wait one further moment to find out." Clumsy in her flippers, she waddled over, reaching up to pull at his arm. "Stop fretting, Finn. It'll be fine."

He let her draw him down for a kiss, but he couldn't stop his hands from clenching into fists. More than he ever had before in his life, he hated what he was.

I am weak, weak to allow her to make this sacrifice. Oath-brother, you would be ashamed of me.

He should be the one giving up everything for her. After all, his own oath-brother, the Pearl Emperor, had left the ocean for the sake of his human mate. At the time, Finn had come close to hating him for being able to abandon the Pearl Throne—abandon *him*—so easily.

Forgive me, oath-brother. I understand now. I would do exactly the same, if she asked.

But she hadn't.

She knew that there was no place for a shark in her warm, joyful pack. Yet they were true mates, unable to be parted. Since he could not join her world, she would sentence herself to his.

And he was too weak to stop her.

"It will be fine," she repeated, breaking away from the kiss at last. Despite her words, a little crease of worry marked her brow. "Now, are you absolutely certain I don't need scuba gear?"

He took her hand, turning it palm-up. "All you need is this."

"Oh, Finn, it's beautiful." Martha held the hinged, filigree locket up to the light, admiring the pattern of curling waves worked into the gold. "This may sound silly, but...is it magic?"

"No. It is just a container." Fighting down sudden nerves, he held out his hand again. "*This* is magic."

Martha's eyes widened at the sight of the pearl in his palm. He was, he secretly had to admit, rather pleased with the way it had turned out. It was an unusual silvery gray, like storm clouds, with flashes of blue-green iridescence where it caught the light.

"That's never a real pearl, is it?" Martha's finger hovered over the shining surface, as if she was scared to touch it. "It's enormous!"

"I would have liked to make it bigger." He eyed it critically, searching once again for any hint of a flaw. It had to be perfect, if he was to entrust his mate to its magic. "But I ran out of time."

Martha's startled gaze jerked up. "You *made* it? How?"

In answer, he put his other hand on top of the pearl, hiding it from sight. Closing his eyes, he rolled it one last time between his palms.

The hidden fire of thermal vents, where the very water burns. The taste of sulfur in his gills. Tiny, glowing creatures who would never know the sun, going about their private, secret lives on the dark sea floor. Unconcerned by his vast silent form soaring through their sky.

Martha gasped as he opened both hands and eyes again. The pearl glowed for a second with the memory he'd wrapped around it, before it faded into the shining surface.

"That's what you were fiddling with the other day!" she exclaimed. "In bed, the morning after the dance. You were making this pearl?"

He nodded, taking the golden locket from her and opening it. "The sea dragons lay claim to many arts. But this one they stole from my people. We are not adept with words. We make our thoughts into pearls instead. They can have great power, depending on what is put into them."

She watched as he fastened the pearl into the locket. "And what did you put in this one?"

"The dreams of a shark." Carefully, he fastened it around her slender neck. "To teach your body what mine already knows."

Her hand flew to the locket. "I'm going to shift into a *shark?*"

Her evident dismay cut him to his heart...though he could not blame her for it. If he was a coyote, he would not want to turn into a shark either.

"No," he said, his voice roughening. "That is beyond my art, and I would not do it even if I could. But it should at least allow you to breathe underwater."

Martha still looked worried, but her back straightened. "Well, what are we waiting for? Let's test it out."

She marched into the surf without another word, dignified as a queen for all her ridiculous, clumsy flippers.

Oh, my mate, my fearless coyote. I am not worthy of your courage.

Nonetheless, he followed, keeping close to her side as she swam out into the bay. Though he had made many pearls for many purposes over his long life, he had never before made one like *this*. He found himself holding his own breath as she ducked under the waves.

She came up laughing, her silver-streaked hair sleek as a seal, eyes shining. She had to splutter up seawater before she could speak. "Oh my Lord, that's *amazing!*"

He let out his breath, his racing heart subsiding at her evident delight. "It pleases you?"

She threw herself at him in answer, wrapping arms and legs around his torso. In the water, they were the same height; she could kiss him freely, without him having to stoop down to her. He tasted sea and salt on her lips as she claimed him with fierce, unrestrained joy.

"Come on," she said, releasing him at last. "Show me your world."

CHAPTER 15

Martha had worried that her inner coyote would be panicked by the unnatural environment. She needn't have feared. Her animal's tail was wagging so hard, it made her own tailbone tingle.

Coyotes were tricksters at heart. And as far as her coyote was concerned, this was the greatest trick ever.

Chase those, her coyote urged as a brilliant shoal of tiny yellow fish swirled past. *And those. And those!*

Martha giggled at her animal's enthusiasm, a stream of silver bubbles rising from her mouth. Succumbing to temptation, she flicked her flippered feet, propelling herself toward the nearest group of fish. They scattered at her approach, exploding in all directions like Fourth of July fireworks.

Better than pigeons! her coyote crowed. *Oh, good mate, excellent mate, to lead us to such fine hunting grounds. Chase that one!*

Martha firmly reined in her inner coyote before the fool animal had her panting after the poor fish like a dog chasing squirrels. She looked for Finn, and discovered him effortlessly keeping pace, a little above her. Though he was still in human form, he didn't seem to be having any trouble breathing underwater either.

Did he make himself a pearl too?

She wanted to ask him, but only bubbles came out when she tried to speak. Catching his eye, she pointed at the locket he'd given her, then gestured at him in silent query.

He shook his head in answer, lifting his chin to show her the gills that had opened in his neck. His hands had become webbed, and his skin had taken on a steely cast, echoing his color in his full shark form. She'd heard of shifters who were able to do partial transformations, though she'd never seen one before.

Just as well he can. He'd beach himself if he shifted this close to shore.

But that meant that these sunlit, teeming waters weren't where he truly belonged. Martha could have spent all day marveling at the jeweled fish—not to mention the crabs and urchins and other creatures she didn't even have names for that were bumbling busily around the sea floor—but they weren't what she'd come here to see.

She wanted to know his true home.

She kicked her feet, heading farther out to sea. She wasn't normally a strong swimmer, but now she soared through the water as easily as a bird through the sky. The saltwater tasted pure and sweet in her mouth, as natural as air. She was weightless. Free.

If this is what it's like to be a shark, I don't know how he can stand to come up onto land.

She'd been expecting the rippling sands of the sea floor to slowly drop away, but instead the transition from shallows to deep sea was sharp as a cliff. She hesitated at the edge of the drop-off, peering down. All she could see below was a murky, blue-green void, fading into blackness.

She took a deep breath, steeling herself—but Finn caught her hand before she could push out into that terrifying emptiness. *Wait,* he mouthed.

He dove into the abyss, barely seeming to need to move a muscle to propel himself through the water. Even though she knew he was perfectly safe, she couldn't help her heart skipping a beat as he disappeared into the dark. More than ever, she wished that they were fully mated, so that they could speak mind-to-mind.

A shockwave of displaced water shook the sea, tumbling her head over heels. By the time she'd righted herself, his iron-gray form was rising back out of the depths.

Even though she'd seen him before, she still caught her breath in awe. He'd been big enough viewed from above, from the safety of the boat. Now that she was actually in the water with him, he seemed to fill the entire sea.

She had to dog-paddle madly to hold her position as he swept past, the currents from his passage tugging at her limbs. His mouth was barely open, but she could still have walked straight between those serried teeth without having to duck her head. If he opened his jaw fully, he could swallow the whole world.

He circled round, slowing as he returned, though he never quite came to a complete stop. He'd warned her that his type of shark needed to keep swimming in order to breathe. This time as he came past, she'd recovered enough presence of mind to swim out to him as they'd agreed.

She caught hold of his towering dorsal fin. Now she understood why he'd insisted she wear diving gloves—his hide was coarse as diamond-grit sandpaper. If she'd been bare-handed, just the slightest brush would have taken the skin off her palms.

Feeling rather like a tick hitching a ride on a bull, she nestled down against his back. She patted him to signal that she was ready.

The great muscles flexed underneath her. Even though she'd been braced for it, she still nearly fell clear off his back as he swept forward. She tightened her grip, water streaming through her hair.

Good *Lord*, he was powerful. From the slow sweeps of his tail, he was barely making an effort, yet his massive form cut through the water with dizzying speed.

She squinted her eyes against the current rushing past. Already, she could barely see the glimmering surface overhead. Deep blue engulfed them. Every stroke of his fins carried her further and further away from everything she'd ever known.

She breathed deeply, water flowing through her mouth, and tried to calm her racing heart. She pressed against his rough back, drawing comfort from his vast strength. She was with her mate. He wouldn't let anything happen to her.

This was where she was meant to be.

He slowed a little, his great head questing from side to side as if sniffing out a scent-trail. Maybe it was the shark-pearl he'd made for her, but Martha could have sworn that she too could taste a difference in the water. A hint of a hidden current; a cold, foreign thread.

I will take you through a Sea Gate, he'd told her. *There is an ancient one here, so old that no one knows which Emperor or Empress first created it. It will take us to Atlantis.*

A thrill went through her at the prospect of more magic. She strained her eyes, looking for—well, in truth, she wasn't quite sure what. A big stone portal, maybe, or a glowing underwater whirlpool.

Instead, the Sea Gate turned out to be much less dramatic than she'd expected. Curving his body, Finn propelled them through a patch of water that looked no different from any other bit. Except then—they were somewhere else.

Martha gasped at the suddenly ice-cold sea. These weren't the gentle, tropical waters of the Caribbean, but the chill depths of the northern Atlantic. She shivered in her wetsuit, instinctively hunkering close to Finn's back, although in truth he was no warmer than the water.

Then she looked down, and forgot all about being cold.

Atlantis gleamed below them. Pearl-white towers rose from the seven tiers of the city, glittering with lights like sunken stars. A golden palace crowned the very tip of the underwater mountain, bright as fire in the dark water. Shimmering bubbles of air enclosed some buildings, but most were left open to the sea.

It was something out of a fairytale. Just like he was.

Finn had gone still beneath her, as if he was trying to judge her reaction. She pressed her body against his back, spreading her arms as wide as she could.

Thank you. Thank you for showing me your home. For letting me in.

Even though she could only span a tiny fraction of his vast form, she knew he'd recognized the hug from the way his taut muscles relaxed. He started swimming down toward the city, his body undulating in slow, easy movements.

Good mate, excellent mate. Her coyote pranced in circles, eager as a pup. *So much to see, so much to sniff! We will run and hunt and dig. And when the pack gathers to chew stories like bones under the moon, this is the one that they will beg us to tell, over and over again.*

Her animal's insatiable curiosity made her smile...but even as she did, a shiver of unease twitched her shoulders. Her coyote thought this was all some grand adventure. A story to tell their grandpups. Her animal didn't yet realize that this was going to be their new home.

New home? Her coyote twitched an ear, as if bothered by a fly. *Nonsense. Our pack is not here.*

Our mate is here, Martha pointed out to her beast.

Of course he is. Because we are here. Her coyote yawned, utterly certain of itself. *And when we go home, he will come with us. Good mate, strong mate. He will help protect our cubs.*

Martha shook her head, knowing better than to try to argue with her stubborn animal. No matter what her beast thought, Arizona was no place for a shark, while a coyote could make itself comfortable just about anywhere.

And her kids were grown-ass adults, as Nita so often reminded her. It was about time she learned to back off a little. She'd still be able to go visit them. This was no different to retiring to Florida or wherever. Just...a little farther off.

If you have to work so hard to convince yourself you're doing the right thing, Manuel had told her on more than one occasion, *you probably aren't.*

Martha squelched the ghostly whisper in her memory. She *was* doing the right thing. Now that she'd seen Atlantis, she was sure of it. How could she ever ask Finn to leave all this shining wonder for the dull, everyday world above the water?

Holding tight to his back, she let her mate carry her home.

∽

By the time they finally made it back to the resort, Martha's legs felt made of lead. She stumbled up the sloping beach, every step a huge effort after the weightless freedom of the sea. But the physical exhaustion of her body was nothing compared to her overwhelmed mind. Her head was so stuffed full of marvels, it was a wonder pearls weren't leaking out of her ears.

The coral-paved streets and intricate mosaics, the underwater gardens and the elegant, shell-white towers…it all blended together in her memory like a dream. And the people, the people! The beauties of the city were nothing compared to the splendor of its inhabitants.

Towering sea dragons with jewel-toned hair, their language more like singing than speech. Quick, fluid seal shifters, so graceful it was a joy just to watch them walk down the street. Orcas and dolphins, walruses and whales…more types of shifter than she'd ever imagined existed.

She'd even met the Pearl Empress—an astonishingly tall, breathtakingly beautiful young woman with calm, sea-blue eyes. Martha hadn't needed the crown on her head or the retinue of knights attending her to know that this was a person of power. Yet the Empress—the ruler of the whole sea!—had smiled at her, taking her hands in her own.

"I hope you will be very happy here." Bizarrely, she'd had a soft Scottish accent, totally unlike the alien tones of every other sea dragon she'd heard that day. "If there's anything I can do to make you feel at home, tell me. I too know what it's like to be a newcomer to Atlantis."

Then the Empress had actually *winked* at her, lowering her voice. "I can assure you, I've at least improved the food down here."

Martha had been too tongue-tied to do more than stammer out a few incoherent words in response. The grandeur, the magic, the glittering sea dragons swimming through the city in their native forms…it was all too overwhelming.

Now she felt like she needed to sit in a darkened room for a week, just to process everything she'd seen. Even her coyote was exhausted, lying belly-up and panting at the bottom of her soul.

"Martha." Finn touched her shoulder, and before she knew what was happening she found herself scooped up in his arms. "I am sorry. We should not have stayed so long."

"It's all right." She leaned gratefully against his broad shoulder. "There was just so much to see. And I still don't think I saw a tenth of it."

"There is plenty of time to see the rest." He fell silent for a moment, carrying her up the beach. "If...you are still certain."

She kissed his neck, tasting the saltwater on his skin. "I still want to be with you, if that's what you mean. And Atlantis is marvelous. Thank you."

Though having seen the place, she had no idea what she was going to *do* there all day. Apart from just gape at everything like a country bumpkin.

We'll figure it out. She snuggled closer into her mate's neck, wrapped in the security of his strong arms. *We'll be together. Everything will be fine, as long as we're together.*

She sighed, a twist of anxiety knotting her gut. Even though she knew she was making the right decision, she still had no idea how she was going to explain this to her pack. To her family. They'd probably think she'd gone stark raving mad when she announced that she was off to live with a shark shifter under the sea.

No sense putting it off. I have to tell them at last.

Finn put her down gently outside the door of her cottage, opening it for her. He started to follow her in, but she put a hand on his chest.

"I need to call my family. Tell them what's going on." She attempted to smile at him. "Probably best if you don't listen in. There's likely to be a lot of yelling."

He hesitated, his eyes shadowed in the moonlight. "Martha-"

"No, go on, shoo." She gave him a firm shove. "This isn't something you can help me with, Finn. It's okay. They'll understand eventually."

I hope, she added to herself, as he reluctantly left. Closing the door, she collapsed back against it with a sigh. She was strongly tempted to just fall into bed and call her family in the morning, but she'd never been one to avoid trouble.

Still, she could at least peel out of her clammy wetsuit and wash the salt out of her hair. She took a shower, for rather longer than was usual, until she could no longer deny to herself that she was just trying to delay the inevitable.

Steeling her nerve, she picked up her cellphone.

26 missed calls, said the screen.

CHAPTER 16

Martha!

Her distress jerked him from sound sleep to combat-readiness in a heartbeat. He snatched up his sword from beside his bed, unsheathing the blade in a single fluid movement as he charged out the door.

He could have followed her scent halfway round the world. This close, it pulled at him stronger than any tide. She needed him, *now*.

And he wasn't there.

Teeth and sword bared, he hurtled over a low barrier with a sign reading *Staff Only*. Lights were flicking on in a long, low building up ahead, sleepy-eyed staff poking their heads out of windows to see what was going on.

"No, it can't wait!" Martha stood outside the staff quarters, fully dressed despite the late hour. "I have to go!"

She seemed to be arguing with an elegant, red-haired woman that he dimly recognized through his blood-rage as Scarlet, the manager of the resort. *Her* scent was strange, ever-shifting, elusive yet powerful. He had no idea what sort of creature she was.

He didn't care. He would rip apart anything that threatened his mate.

"Martha!" he roared.

"Finn!" She spun, hurling herself at him. "I have to leave, right now!"

"Then we are leaving." He pulled her close to his side, his sword raised and ready. "And I will kill anyone who stands in our way."

Scarlet made an impatient sound under her breath. "Put that thing away before someone gets hurt. As I was saying, Mrs. Hernandez, the next plane isn't scheduled to arrive at the island until Saturday. I can't get it here any faster than that."

"I can't wait until Saturday. I have to get home!"

"Martha, what is wrong?" He didn't lower his blade yet.

"It's Roddie, my youngest son. He's gone missing. Nita called and called, she's frantic with worry. He was last seen on rattlesnake territory and half the pack is baying for war and she doesn't know how to settle them…" Martha took a deep breath, her jaw setting again into the firm line he'd come to know so well. "I have to go," she repeated, more calmly. "Scarlet, please, there must be something you can do."

"There might be something leaving from the mainland." The resort manager took out her cellphone, frowning down at the screen. "Yes, there's a flight out in four hours. Bastian?"

A man with the unmistakable smoke-and-metal scent of a dragon shifter stepped forward from the watching group of staff. "I can fly her there in time. We'll have to leave soon, though."

"Travis, Breck, go help pack up Mrs. Hernandez's cases," Scarlet ordered. "Mrs. Hernandez, I'll book your ticket now."

"Two tickets."

All eyes turned to him.

"I think airport security might object to the sword," Tex murmured from somewhere in the crowd. "Though I'd love to see them try to take it off him."

He ignored the whispers, focused only on Martha. "I am coming with you."

For a second, he imagined he saw a flare of relief in her eyes—but then she pushed him away. "No. This is my pack. My responsibility."

"And you are mine. I am coming with you."

"You *can't*, Finn!" She retreated a step, holding up both hands as if to stop him from following. "They don't even know about you! How on earth would I explain why a shark's interested in coyote business?"

"You could tell them the truth." The instant, slight shake of her head cut him to his heart, but he persisted anyway. "That I am your mate."

"I can't! Not now, not after this!" Martha's face crumpled, her mouth trembling. "She was calling and calling all day, Finn, and *I wasn't here!*"

Her words took his own away, as surely as if she'd slit his throat.

She hadn't been there for her pack…because she'd been in Atlantis. With him.

"I never should have left them," Martha whispered, tears streaking her face. "I can't do this. I'm sorry, Finn. I'm so, so sorry."

She turned away. And he could do nothing but watch her go.

CHAPTER 17

"Ma!" Nita flung herself into Martha's arms the instant she stepped out of the airport gate. Martha hugged her eldest tight, feeling her shake.

"It's okay, sweetheart," Martha whispered, rocking her as if she was just a baby again. "I'm back now. Everything's going to be just fine."

She breathed in Nita's familiar scent. Desert and dry grass, warm fur and sunbaked rock, just as always. The scent of pack, of family, of home. Yet she had a strange, nagging sense that something was different.

That something was missing.

"Where are the kids?" she asked, wondering if that was what was bothering her. "And Xo? Did you come all by yourself?"

"Yeah. I kind of suspected I might fall apart. Didn't want an audience." Nita released her at last, stepping back. She swiped the palm of her hand quickly across her eyes, and essayed a tremulous smile. "Some alpha I turned out to be. The first hint of trouble, and I'm howling for you like a lost cub."

"There's no shame in asking for help, honey. I should have been here in the first place."

Despite her words, double guilt stabbed her heart. She shouldn't have left home…but she shouldn't have left Finn either. Especially not like that, all in a rush, half-mad with panic.

She felt hollow inside. She'd left her heart buried in Shifting Sands.

She set her shoulders. Her family needed her. That was all that mattered now.

"Tell me what's happened since we last talked," she said to Nita. "Anyone been able to pick up any scent of Roddie?"

Nita shook her head, taking her suitcase from her. "Not apart from that one trace I told you about, over on the far side of rattlesnake country. It's been all I can do to hold Diego and Ethan back from launching a raid."

"Those hell-raisers." Martha clicked her tongue. "Well, your brothers had better listen to *me*, if they know what's good for them. I remember the last war with the snakes. I'm not having another one. Have you tried talking to the rattlers?"

"Didn't seem to be much point."

"What makes you say that?"

Nita looked at her as if she'd started barking. "Because they're *snakes*, Ma. Since when do we listen to snakes?"

Maybe since I started sleeping with a shark. Oh, Finn.

"Anyway," Nita continued, "there was snake-stink all over Roddie's trail, enough to choke on. They had something to do with him disappearing, without a doubt."

If that was true, then even she wouldn't be able to stop her hotheaded pack from declaring vengeance. The bad blood between coyotes and rattlesnakes stretched back longer than anyone could remember. They were always just a spark away from a wildfire.

"I didn't know what to do, Ma," Nita said in a very small voice. "Thanks for coming back. I'm sorry you had to cut your vacation short."

Martha hugged her again. "You did the right thing, honey. This is where I'm supposed to be."

She buried her nose in Nita's dark hair again. Desert and dry grass, fur and rock…

But no salt.

Home didn't smell like home anymore. Not without the sea.

Her coyote howled, desolate and alone.

CHAPTER 18

"We will not tolerate these incursions into our territories!" The Lady of Seals slammed one fist down onto the shell-inlaid surface of the Sea Council table, her liquid brown eyes blazing with anger. "If you will not control your kin, *honorable* Lord Orca, then we shall control them for you!"

"I will not allow the wild whales to be starved." The killer whale shifter's bared teeth were white as his hair, a stark contrast to his jet-black skin. "What would you have me do, tell the non-shifter orcas to eat krill? Seals are their natural prey. You have no right to protect your kin at the expense of mine!"

"Lady Seal, Lord Orca, peace." The Pearl Empress rubbed her forehead, looking weary. "We have been at this for hours, and you are still simply going in circles. Master Shark? What are your thoughts?"

Warm fur and laughing eyes. Sunlight and sand.

All his thoughts were only for her. But his Empress had called on him. With an effort, he forced himself to focus on the quarreling lords, though he had no heart for it.

He had no heart at all, anymore.

He rose. "My people shall claim the contested territory. And *both* your kinds are *our* natural prey."

The Empress blinked across the table at him, as the council chamber erupted.

"You can't do that-"

"Utterly unacceptable-"

The Lady Seal and the Lord Orca were finally united in agreement about one thing, at least. Their overlapping voices rose in outrage.

"Continue speaking," he said flatly, his harsh voice cutting through the babble, "and I shall eat you."

The Lord Orca's mouth closed with an audible click. The Lady of Seals, younger and less experienced, looked mortally affronted.

"How *dare* you-" she began.

He looked at her. She fell silent, shrinking back into her seat.

The Empress stood, causing a mass scraping of chairs as every other member of the Sea Council hastened to rise as well. "We will take a short recess. Master Shark, *a word.*"

The rest of the Sea Council gratefully fled. The Empress motioned the on-duty guards out as well, though the Royal Consort stayed by her side, as ever.

The Empress waited until the three of them were alone, then whirled to face him, her hands on her hips. "What on earth was that?"

"You wished me to resolve their dispute, Your Majesty."

"Not with your teeth!"

"I am a shark. How did you expect me to resolve it?"

She raked her hand through her curly hair, knocking her crown askew. "With tact and subtlety and just the barest hint of threat, the way that you have always done. Master Shark, what is wrong with you?"

He stared at her, impassive. She knew full well what was wrong. He'd been forced to tell her, in the bare minimum of words, when he'd unexpectedly returned to Atlantis.

The Empress winced, biting her lip. "I'm sorry, Master Shark. That was thoughtless of me. Look, are you sure you don't want to take some time off?"

"I took one vacation at your bidding, Your Majesty," he said stiffly. "I will not take another. Now allow me to return to my duty."

"No."

Both he and the Empress looked around at the Royal Consort. The towering sea dragon met their stares steadily, his indigo eyes cool and unreadable.

"When last I checked, *Royal Consort*," the Master Shark gritted out through clenched teeth, "'Emperor' was not among your many titles."

"But I am still the Imperial Champion, responsible for the Empress's well-being." The sea dragon folded his arms across his broad chest, armored vambraces catching the light. "And you have become a liability."

Blind fury filled him, the first emotion he'd felt since his mate had walked away. "*You* are the one who insisted I was needed here!"

"The Empress needs the Master Shark!" The sea dragon's own voice rose, scornful harmonics scratching around his words. "Not some hollow, hungering husk. What good are you to her like this, *coward?*"

His control snapped. If he'd had his sword, it would already have been in the sea dragon's heart. He lunged for the Royal Consort barehanded, murderous with rage.

The sea dragon was less than half his age, and the finest swordsman in the sea—but he was the Master Shark. He barely felt the blow the Royal Consort landed on his face, returning one of his own that sent the younger man staggering.

"STOP!" The Empress's shout stopped them both in their tracks—quite literally.

Her magic froze the blood in his veins, holding him motionless. All the seas were hers to command, and he was as much a part of her domain as the waves or the tides. Darkness encroached on the edge of his vision as his heart stuttered.

The Empress held them for a moment longer before releasing them. Both he and the Royal Consort fell to their knees, fight forgotten as they gasped for breath.

"Have you lost your mind, John?" the Empress demanded of her mate. "What do you think you're doing?"

"What I wish someone had done for me," the sea dragon knight panted. Despite the blood running down his chin, his mouth crooked in a wry smile. "Knocking some sense into his thick skull."

"*Men*," the Empress muttered under her breath. "Get up, the pair of you. Master Shark, much as I disagree with John's methods, he's right. You're destroying yourself. You have to go to your mate."

The Royal Consort leaped to his feet with the smooth agility of youth. A rather challenging gleam still in his eyes, he leaned down to offer his hand. The Master Shark stared at it for a second...and then clasped it. He allowed the sea dragon to pull him to his feet.

The brief fight had ripped away the numbness in his soul. The Royal Consort was right. He was a coward. He had fled from his mate, out of fear of being hurt further.

But nothing could hurt more than her absence.

Nonetheless, he hesitated. "But I am needed here."

"Would you like me to strike you again?" the Royal Consort inquired, in tones of utmost politeness.

The Empress elbowed her mate, though a smile tugged at her full lips. "I think we've already established that you're not entirely yourself at the moment, Master Shark. And Martha will be feeling the same way. What sort of pain do you think *she's* in right now?"

Her words struck him harder than the Royal Consort's fist had. The mere thought of Martha feeling even a fraction of this agony...

"She has the comfort of her pack," he said, trying to convince himself. "They are enough for her. And...and she did not want me to follow."

The Royal Consort's eyebrows rose. "Does it truly take so little to turn aside a shark?"

"What does your heart tell you, Master Shark?" the Empress said softly.

He reached out for his mate's blood-scent...and knew that no matter what she had said then, she was calling to him now.

"My Empress." He went to both knees before her, bowing his head in the full formal show of respect, as befitted someone seeking a great boon. "I cannot be myself again without my mate. But she will not come here."

"Then we will have to learn to do without you." The Empress put a hand on his face, lifting his chin so he met her gaze. "Master Shark, if the Pearl Empire demands that we sacrifice our souls to it, then it does not deserve to exist. It has to be bigger than any one of us. Even you. Even me."

He looked up at her for a long, long moment.

His oath-brother's daughter. Human and sea dragon, the child of two worlds.

"Your father," he said, "would be very proud of you."

Tears brimmed in her eyes. Leaning down, she kissed his cheek.

"Go to your mate, Master Shark," she whispered.

"Finn," he replied, rising. "My name is Finn."

CHAPTER 19

"If we'd seen your pup, then he wouldn't be missing." The rattlesnake leader's lips stretched in a grin, showing off his inch-long, needle-sharp canines. "You'd know exactly where he was. You'd be carving his name on a stone to mark his grave."

"Don't you point those fangs at me, young man." Martha folded her arms, shooting him a withering stare. "I've seen far scarier teeth than yours, thank you very much. Hiss all you want, but we know someone of yours knows something about Roddie. Now, I've asked you nicely who that might be. You going to make me ask again?"

The snake shifter's eyes were hidden behind sunglasses, but Martha was fairly certain they flicked to her bristling escort. Her three older sons were in coyote form, unconvincingly disguised with collars and bandanas to look like ordinary dogs. Nita held her brothers' leashes. Given the way her daughter was growling, Martha was somewhat regretting not putting *her* on a lead too.

The rattlesnake himself seemed to have come alone—though Martha wouldn't have placed any bets on that. A snake was a heck of a lot easier to hide than a coyote, even in the dusty 7-11 parking lot they'd picked as neutral ground. He could have a whole passel of his kin within spitting distance.

If he did, he wasn't calling them out yet. The young snake leaned against his motorbike in a way that he probably meant to come off as cool and menacing, but which screamed uneasy defensiveness to Martha's experienced eye.

"Last time I saw your boy was Wednesday. We caught him sniffing round our borders again, and sent him howling back to momma. Told him it was his final warning." The snake shifter's lip curled. "He tell you about that?"

Did he? Martha asked Nita telepathically down the pack bond.

No, Nita sent back, her mental tone grim. *Sorry, Ma. Guess I should have sniffed his laundry to check for snake-stink.*

"I apologize for his bad manners," Martha said to the snake. "I should have taught him better. But he's my youngest son—my baby boy. Think how worried *your* ma would be if you disappeared. Surely you can be neighborly enough to point us in the right direction?"

The snake shifter spat in the dirt. "Told you all I know. Now get out."

Her sons' growls kicked up a notch. Martha could tell just as well as them that the rattlesnake was lying through his fangs. He did know something, and he'd rather bleed on the sand than tell it to her.

Heaven save us from insecure young alphas itching to prove themselves.

Of course, thirty years back *she'd* been that rash young pup desperate to keep face in front of her pack. It had taken an all-out war to knock some sense into her fool head.

She could only pray that the young rattlesnake was a faster learner than she'd been.

"I don't want any trouble between our people," she said, letting her voice harden. "Your old man, God rest his soul, kept his side of the treaty, and I aim to make sure my pack keeps ours. But in order to do that, I need you to cooperate with me."

The rattlesnake showed his fangs again. "Don't you threaten me, you old bi-"

Fortunately for the snake shifter, his words were cut off by Nita's sudden shriek. "Roddie!"

Martha whirled, rattlesnake forgotten as the wind carried her baby boy's scent to her too. A second later, his gangling, hangdog form stepped round the corner of the 7-11. He wasn't alone, either. A copper-skinned girl with waist-length black hair clung to his arm, a defiant look on her face. And behind them-

"*Finn?*" Martha gasped.

He loomed behind the sheepish pair like a cop bringing a couple of juvenile delinquents home to face the music. Martha could scarce believe her eyes…but her nose didn't lie.

His fierce salt scent filled the gaping void in her heart. She hadn't realized how much she'd been hurting, until she wasn't.

"Oh, Finn," she breathed.

She would have run to him despite her goggling kids, but the rattlesnake shifter moved first. He pelted for the girl, all cool forgotten.

"Celia!" he yelled, his voice cracking with relief. Half a dozen snakes poured after him, emerging from under dumpsters. "You're okay!"

"More than okay," the girl said, holding up her left hand. A wedding band glinted from her finger. "I'm married."

"You're *what?*" The snake shifter whirled on Roddie, fangs bared. "What the hell have you done to my little sister?"

"What the hell have you done to my little brother?" Nita yelled at the girl.

In all the fuss and confusion, Martha only had eyes for one person. Finn circled unnoticed around the arguing snakes and coyotes, moving silently to her side. He stopped slightly out of arms'-reach, as if he was just a casual acquaintance.

"Hello," he said quietly.

Something about his appearance struck her as utterly ludicrous. She had to gape at him for a moment before she worked out what was different about him.

"You're wearing a shirt," she said, stupidly.

His teeth gleamed. "I could remove it, if you prefer."

"Yes, please. I mean, no. Later. What?" Her human mind was

moving like molasses, while her coyote was mad with joy. "Finn, what are you *doing* here?"

He tilted his head. "I decided to take another vacation."

"So soon? Your Empress didn't mind? How long can you stay?"

"Forever." His voice was the barest breath. "If you will have me."

"And what about him, Roddie?" Nita was demanding of her brother, as she jerked her thumb at Finn. The rattlesnake shifter was also eying the massive shark shifter warily. "Why's he with you?"

"He tracked me and Celia down in Vegas, by following our blood-scent or something. He made us come back." Roddie grimaced. "He's kind of hard to say 'no' to."

"We ran away because we knew none of you would understand," the rattlesnake girl said, clutching him even tighter. "But not even your hired shark can separate us. We're true mates, like it or not."

"He's a *shark?*" Nita looked as though none of this was making any sense whatsoever. "Ma, did you have something to do with this? Who is this man?"

The question hung in the air. Finn said nothing, expression impassive as a rock, giving her the space to answer as she chose.

Martha took Finn's hand. His rough fingers closed around hers.

And she knew that they were both where they were meant to be.

She lifted her chin proudly, smiling at her family. "He's my mate."

EPILOGUE

Martha let out her breath as a grinning Roddie swept up his bride and kissed her thoroughly, to howls of approval. "Well, that went more smoothly than I was expecting."

"You feared they would not accept her?" The flickering light of the bonfire caught the stark planes of Finn's strong forehead and jaw as he watched the pack gather around the newly-mated pair.

"Some of the older pack members are still having a hard time getting their heads around a rattlesnake joining us." There *were* some hisses mingled in with the howls, but she was fairly certain they were coming from the snakes lurking at the edges of the crowd, and were meant kindly. "But since the youngsters are busy changing the world, all us old sticks will just have to learn to change with it."

Finn chuckled, pulling her closer against his side. "I do not think you can cast all the blame on the young, when it comes to changes."

She snuggled into him, the coolness of his bare skin refreshing in the hot, humid night. He was wearing his formal armor again, in honor of the occasion. Given that most of the pups at the party were haring around with their butts hanging out, shifting freely between two feet and four—or none, in the case of the snakes—his bare torso wasn't going to raise any eyebrows. Though Martha *had* noticed more than one woman there sneaking a glance or three at his endless pecs.

Let them admire him. Her inner coyote was smug as a cat in cream. *He is ours.*

"All right, all right!" Nita leaped back up onto the impromptu platform—constructed out of a couple of planks laid across some beer kegs—in front of the bonfire. "Settle down. This isn't the only petition tonight, after all."

Martha felt Finn's muscles go rigid against her. "*You* aren't nervous, are you?" she murmured.

From the stony blankness settling over his face, he was. Quite a few coyotes drew back from him as he walked through the crowd. Martha couldn't entirely blame them. Finn looked more like a man contemplating a massacre than a mating.

Even standing on the beer barrels, Nita still had to tip her chin up to look him in the eye. "Who seeks to join the Ochre Rock pack?" she asked formally.

"My name is Finn." His rasping voice carried clearly over the expectant hush. Even the crickets seemed to fall silent to hear him. "Formerly the Master Shark, and the Voice of the Pearl Empress. In days long gone, I was the King of Teeth, ruler of all the sharks of the sea."

A little ripple went through the crowd, from those who hadn't heard his titles before. Nita let the murmurs die down before she continued. "And what do you offer the pack, Finn? Why should we accept you?"

"I am a good hunter. I can follow my prey halfway across the world."

"I wish he couldn't," Roddie called, to scattered laughter.

"I know how to fight." The bonfire gilded the edges of Finn's armor as he glanced at the small knot of gathered rattlesnakes. "And, more importantly, how *not* to fight. I know how to keep the peace, even between those who are natural enemies. These are the skills I offer to the pack."

Nita turned to the crowd, her hands on her hips. "Well, Ochre Rock? Does he offer us enough?"

"No!" every coyote howled back gleefully.

Martha was very glad Finn had just seen Celia go through this exact same hazing, because otherwise she would have put even odds on him having a heart attack on the spot. As it was, he stiffened, every muscle knotting tight. He looked on the verge of murder—a sure sign of extreme nerves.

Nita pursed her lips. "Well then, how shall we make him prove himself?"

Celia had been challenged to demonstrate a rattlesnake's venom by cussing out her brother. With a gleam in her eye, she'd delivered a three-minute stream of inventive invective that had blistered the alpha snake's scaly hide and made every mother present clap hands over the ears of their offspring. Even Martha's twin boys had been impressed.

I wonder what they'll make him do?

"Eat a whole cow!" Martha's grandson Manny yelled out.

"We're trying to give him a challenge, not a snack," Nita said, sparking more laughter. "Anything else?"

"Make him walk barefoot across the desert!"

"Clear out the cacti from Ten Acres!"

Finn's taut shoulders eased down a bit as the suggestions kept coming, each more preposterous than the last. When someone proposed that he beat all comers in a dance-off, he caught her eye. His mouth quirked slightly.

Martha grinned back, shaking her head in response. She hadn't put her pack up to *that* one.

Wouldn't they be surprised.

"Make him wrestle all the other men," Martha's youngest sister suggested, her amber eyes wicked. "In mud."

This proposal met with overwhelming feminine approval. Unfortunately, it was unanimously vetoed by the male members of the pack.

"Well, Ochre Rock, since it seems you all can't come to agreement, it falls to me as acting alpha to set the challenge." Nita turned back to

Finn, her expression turning serious. "We have welcomed a rattlesnake into our pack today…but a shark? Our new sister Celia at least was born here, and has the desert in her blood. Now we are asked to accept someone into the pack who is as foreign to us as the sea. Someone who cannot shift and hunt with us under the full moon."

Even though she was pretty certain Nita wouldn't *really* reject Finn outright, Martha's stomach still twisted. She made herself bite her tongue. She'd named her daughter acting alpha, and started handing over the day-to-day responsibilities of the pack. She had to trust that Nita knew what she was doing.

"That is a huge thing to ask indeed," Nita continued. She looked every inch the strong, serious alpha. "It demands an appropriate challenge in response. So I will lay on you a task that will not be simply done once and quickly forgotten, but a service that you must perform for this pack every single day."

Finn had gone as still as stone. Martha held her own breath.

"Finn, if you would join the Ochre Rock pack, this is what you must do." Nita's voice rang out in the utter silence. "Make my mother happy."

His eyes met hers. Tears sprang into the corners of her own as the entire pack erupted into howls of approval.

"And keep her too busy to stick her nose into other people's business!" her son Diego yelled out over the ruckus.

"I thought the challenge had to be possible," Finn said dryly, causing a wave of fresh laughter.

"That it does. So we'll go with just making her happy." Nita raised her eyebrows at Finn. "Well, shark? Willing to face this challenge?"

Finn bowed his head, grave as a knight of old accepting some perilous quest. "I am."

"Then, as acting alpha…" Nita flung her arms around his broad neck, grinning from ear to ear. "Welcome to the pack, Finn of Ochre Rock."

Martha hung back as the other pack members surged forward, converging on Finn like a laughing, noisy tide. With every welcoming hug, every hand-shake and back-slap, the warm glow in her heart grew, until it shone brighter than the bonfire behind his towering form.

He was part of the pack. Now, he truly was her mate.

And soon she would be his too.

"I was so nervous!" Nita appeared at her side, wiping the back of her hand across her forehead. "I'm sweating like a hog. You always made it look so easy to address the pack. Did I do okay?"

"You were just perfect." Martha hugged her daughter, half-laughing, half-crying. "Oh, honey. That was perfect. You're going to make an amazing alpha."

"Still got a lot to learn." Breaking the embrace, Nita snagged a beer from her passing wife. "So promise you won't go anywhere."

"Now, you know I can't do that yet. Chevelon Canyon Lake is no more than a puddle for him." Martha jerked her thumb at the quiet, rippling waters lapping at the shore beyond the bonfire. It was the biggest body of water in the pack's territory, but it still wasn't nearly deep enough for a megalodon. "The poor man has to take an eight hour drive just to be able to shift. I can't ask him to do that long-term."

Nita sighed, hunching her shoulders. "Well, guess I should be grateful you're just considering retiring to San Diego rather than Atlantis. But I'll miss you, Ma."

"Don't worry." Martha cocked an eyebrow at her, grinning. "I promise I'll call."

∼

He'd never been touched so much in his entire life. Every time he turned, there was some new relative wanting to clap him on the shoulder or squeeze his arm. He swam through a sea of smiling, upturned faces and warm hands.

I did not know I was so hungry, to be so full.

"Here, Finn." One of Martha's identical twin sons—Diego or Ethan, he still had a hard time telling them apart—handed him a bottle. "This calls for a toast."

He accepted the drink, a little warily. It had become something of a game over the last few weeks for the younger men of the pack to try to find an alcoholic beverage he found palatable. He was still somewhat suspicious that the revoltingly foamy, insipid drink they'd called 'beer' had been some sort of elaborate practical joke.

He took a cautious sip. It was at least inoffensive. "Mildly refreshing."

Diego, or possibly Ethan, looked around at the watching young men hopefully. "That close enough?"

"I think with two hundred bucks at stake, you'll have to do better than that, Diego," one of them replied. "What is it, anyway?"

"Straight bourbon." Diego took the bottle back, looking at it mournfully. "Described as 'mildly refreshing.' No-one is *ever* going to win the bet at this rate."

Sid, the rattlesnake alpha, had been watching from the shadows just outside the circle of coyotes. They bristled a little as he stepped forward. The young snake ignored the glares, though his tense shoulders showed that he was aware of them.

"I gather that there's some sort of bet?" He held up a hip flask.

Diego's eyes narrowed. "Don't know if you should trust anything that comes from a snake's hands, Finn."

In answer, he took the flask. Without hesitation or a word, he raised it to his lips.

There was a long pause.

"Now *that*," he said, lowering the flask again, "is a drink."

Sid grinned, showing his fangs, as the coyotes erupted into groans and recriminations. The alpha snake held out a hand. Grumbling, the coyotes started pulling out their wallets.

"Did you really enjoy that, or is this just a shark's sense of humor?" Diego asked Finn suspiciously as he counted out bills.

He tipped the flask upside-down. Not a drop ran out. "I will drink more to prove it, if you would like."

Sid's yellow eyes widened. He had slit pupils, like a cat. Much like shark shifters, many snakes had a hard time appearing fully human.

"You just drank half a flask of snakebite, and you're asking for *more*?" he choked out.

"It is pleasantly bracing." Finn handed the flask back to him. "Perhaps we could drink together again, some other time. There are matters I would discuss with you."

The young rattlesnake looked wary. "Like what?"

"Among other things," Finn smiled, showing his teeth, "where to find discreet dentists."

"Hate to break up all this male bonding, but my man has to start making good on his promise now." Martha had appeared at his elbow. She tugged at his arm. "Come on, Finn. Dancing's about to start."

With a parting nod, he allowed her to draw him away. The heat of her hand was more intoxicating than the burn of the snakebite. He fought down an urge to pull her away from the party and into the dark woods. Much as he was enjoying the warmth and laughter of the evening…she still was not fully his mate.

Soon, he promised himself. *Soon.*

"What was all that about back there?" she asked him, as they headed toward the bonfire.

"Diplomacy," he replied, smiling. "Old habits die hard."

She nipped teasingly at his arm. "No working tonight. This is an evening for fun. Enjoy it."

He stopped, turning her to face him. Tilting her head, he ducked to plant a slow, lingering kiss on the side of her neck. Very gently, he pressed his teeth against her warm skin, and felt her shiver from head to toe in response.

"I shall," he breathed.

From her dark eyes and the hitch in her breath, she too was contemplating the possibilities of some private, secluded glade. Nonetheless she shook herself.

"Later," she said firmly, taking his hand again. "Come dance with me first. No one believed me when I told them you can salsa. I want to see the looks on their faces."

He responded by pulling her into the dance hold. Laughing, she let him spin her around, her eyes shining in the firelight.

Hand in hand, they danced the rest of the way across the clearing, to where their family waited to welcome them.

~

"May I cut in?"

Panting with exertion, Martha looked up—and lost her breath entirely.

The Pearl Empress, ruler of all the shifters of the sea, smiled down at her. Her towering, indigo-haired mate stood behind the sea dragon queen, face solemn but eyes gleaming.

From the startled look on Finn's face, he hadn't been expecting them either. He started to go down to one knee, but the Empress stopped him with a gesture.

"We're not here on official business. Just to dance at your mating celebration." The Empress raised her eyebrows at Martha. "If you'll let me borrow your mate for a few minutes?"

Martha relinquished Finn to her. He still had a slightly stunned look on his face as he took his Empress's hands. They whirled away, the Empress falling easily into step with the music.

"I am afraid I am not one for dancing," the Empress's mate said to her, bowing a little. "But perhaps you will walk with me?"

Martha took his offered arm. She racked her brain for how he'd introduced himself back in Atlantis, but all that she could remember was that it had been *long*. "Uh, I'm afraid I forgot your title."

"Royal Consort of the Pearl Empress, Imperial Champion for the Pearl Throne, Knight-Poet of the First Water, and Firefighter for the East Sussex Fire and Rescue Service." He smiled down at her. He was even taller than Finn. "But you can call me John."

"Firefighter?" she couldn't help asking, as they headed away from the dancers and toward the peace of the lake shore. "Really?"

He inclined his head in confirmation. "It is a long story. But if you are ever in England, I would very much like to introduce you to my comrades on Alpha Team. One of them is…somewhat akin to your

Master Shark. Born to a position of power, and isolated by his unique nature. But you, I think, would not be intimidated by him."

"I'd love to. Um, though don't hold your breath. I've already had one exotic vacation this year, and England's kind of a long way away."

He shot her a somewhat mysterious glance, one corner of his mouth twitching up. "Perhaps it may be closer than you think."

She narrowed her eyes at him. "How *did* you get here tonight, John? Sea dragons don't fly, as far as I'm aware."

"No more than sharks do." He glanced back at the dancers, his expression sobering. "If I may ask…is he happy here?"

"Think so." A sudden fear seized her heart. "That's not why the two of you are here, is it? To ask him to go back?"

John shook his head, the gold charms braided into his hair catching the firelight. "On my honor, we are not. And we would not. His days of service are done. She came to give him some gifts, that is all."

Martha let out her breath, slowly. "Good. Just be warned, if I ever get the feeling you all are nagging at him, I'll put a flea in your ear. And any of my kids will tell you that you don't want *that*."

"I will consider myself warned." He chuckled. "Though we may need to ask you to berate the Sea Council. *They* are begging the Empress to bring back the Master Shark."

"What?" Martha's eyebrows shot up. "I thought the other sea lords hated him?"

"Oh yes. But at least there was only one of him." John's white teeth gleamed against his dark skin, his smile rather predatory for all that it wasn't as sharp-edged as Finn's. "Now there are five. The Empress reinstated the Council of Teeth, giving them all official positions as part of the Sea Council."

Martha smirked. "Five Shark Lords instead of one Master Shark. Sounds like a fair trade to me. Though I'd have liked to have seen the sea lords' faces when she announced it."

"I am surprised you did not hear the screams from here." He gazed out at the reflection of the moon in the lake. "My Empress wished to speak with your mate…but I came to speak with you. I would ask you for a favor, if you would permit it."

Martha blinked at him. She couldn't imagine this strapping young man needing anything from *her*. "What kind of favor?"

"I am the Imperial Champion, and my greatest and foremost duty is to protect my mate." His voice softened, his pride and love clear. "She is strong—stronger than even she knows—but even the strongest leader sometimes needs guidance from those older and richer in experience. She would never disturb the peace that he has earned…but I would ask you to visit Atlantis, from time to time. For her sake."

"That we'll do, and gladly." Martha smiled up at him. "It'll take us a little while to find the balance that works, how we're going to live our lives from now on. I've still got my hands too tight on the reins here to let go easy. But if a Master Shark can learn to step back and let others have their turn driving, I guess an old coyote can do the same. You'll be seeing us in Atlantis, never fear."

He bowed to her, like a knight from a fairytale. "We will be honored."

"Ready to go, John?" The Empress walked toward them, Finn at her side. He had a slightly strange look on his face, as if he was trying to process something. There was a black pearl around his neck, strung on a silver chain, that hadn't been there before.

Martha went to her mate, taking his hand. "All okay?"

He nodded at her, but it was the Empress he addressed. "I will think on it. Expect to hear from me soon."

The Empress touched the pearl at his throat. "You know how to reach me. Thank you, Master—that is, Finn."

The pair waded into the lake. A wave of displaced water surged over the shore as they shifted, their human shapes blurring into the impossibly large, sinuous forms of sea dragons.

The Empress was black as the night, every scale shining like the pearl around Finn's neck; John, a deep, rich indigo, the exact shade of his hair in human form. The water closed over their jeweled backs.

"What did she want to give you?" Martha asked Finn, as they

watched the V-shaped ripples head toward the center of the lake. "That pearl?"

He nodded, touching it. "It is for scrying. I used to have a similar one, when I was the Voice of the Empress. It will allow me to speak to her, when I wish, using the surface of a pool of water."

"Sounds handy. And what's this thing you told her you'd think about?"

He hesitated. "She...told me some news. The Pearl Empire will have a new heir, this time next year."

"Oh! They're having a baby?"

"Yes." His gaze tracked the distant ripples of the underwater sea dragons. "She asked if I would be the child's champion. Godfather, I think you would call it."

She squeezed his hand. "Sounds like quite an honor."

"It is." He looked down at her, his deep-set eyes shadowed. "But...it is a tie to Atlantis. I did not know whether you would approve of that."

She nestled closer to his side. "Of course I do. It's where you come from, Finn. I don't want you to never see your home again."

He kissed the top of her head. "You are my home."

"Oh, you." Martha narrowed her eyes. The ripples on the water had vanished, suspiciously abruptly. "Hey, where did they go? For that matter, how *did* they get here?"

His lips curved in a slight, mysterious smile. "Do you have your pearl?"

"Of course I do." Martha touched the golden locket that she always wore around her neck. "Why?"

Without a further word, he waded out into the lake. Turning, he held out his hand to her.

Martha glanced back at the distant bonfire, with the silhouettes of their pack gathered around it. The party was starting to die down now, parents gathering up dozing children and carrying them off to blankets under the stars. A few other couples were quietly slipping away into the trees, hand-in-hand. Soft laughter carried on the warm night air.

Their pack was safe, and happy. For a few hours at least, they wouldn't be missed.

Her pulse rose in anticipation as she joined Finn, the lake water lapping around her thighs. Taking her hand, he drew her deeper, until the lake lifted her off her feet and into his waiting arms.

He bore her up in the water, her back to his front, his calm, strong heartbeat echoing in her own chest. Tipping back her head, she stretched out her limbs, letting the water stream like ribbons through her spread fingers. The cloudless night was ablaze with stars. Weightless in the water, she could scarce tell where the lake ended and the sky began. She floated through eternity, wrapped in her mate's embrace.

"Ready?" he said softly into her ear.

"For what?" she started to say, but he was already ducking them under the water. Her words were lost in bubbles, the pearl around her neck glowing as its magic took hold.

The water of the lake tasted different than the sea had; a hot, muggy June day rather than clear winter air. It was murkier too, so that she could barely see Finn's pale form swimming beside her. She kept a tight hold of his hand as he drew her down into the depths.

And then-

She gasped in shock at the sudden salt tang in her mouth. The green-brown lake waters turned to crystal-clear turquoise. The unmistakable murmur of the open sea filled her ears as they floated up to the surface.

The instant their heads broke into air, she flung her arms around his neck, whooping with delight. She could feel him smiling against her lips as she kissed him.

"A Sea Gate?" she said, when they broke apart at last. "Why didn't you *tell* me there was one in our lake?"

His deep, rasping laugh vibrated through her bones. "Because there wasn't, until tonight. The Empress made it. The third gift she came to give us."

She hugged him tight, tears of joy mingling with the saltwater on her cheeks. "So now the sea is always just a short swim away. We can stay with the pack, and still visit Atlantis whenever we want, and —oh, *Finn.*"

"Not just Atlantis." He turned her in the water, pointing. "Look."

An island rose out of the sea, its low peak crowned by stars. The breeze carried the faint scent of jasmine across the waves. In the distance, she could just about make out a few scattered lights, nestled above the wide, sweeping bay.

All the breath sighed out of her. "Shifting Sands?"

He kissed the side of her neck. "It seemed only appropriate."

The slight pressure of his teeth against her skin made her toes curl in the water. "How fast can you swim?"

The answer, it turned out, was 'astonishingly fast.' Before she knew it, he was carrying her out of the surf. She sighed again in delight as she recognized the tiny, hidden cove with its tumbling waterfall.

The place where she'd first shown him her coyote. The place where he'd first given her his smile.

"Oh yes," she breathed. "Here."

The white sands still held the warm heat of day. He lay her down on them, covering her body with his own. She closed her eyes as he kissed her gently, languidly, as though they had all the time in the world.

And oh, they did, they did.

The sea murmured in soft applause as they took their time. She was intimately familiar by now with every hard plane of his body, yet awed delight still rose in her like the tide every time she touched him.

She ran her fingers over the curve of his chest, down the hollow of his spine. She traced the tracks of old scars with her tongue. So many battles, so many long hard years, and yet he had fought his way home to her arms.

He stroked her in return; the laughter-lines at the corners of her eyes, the callouses on her fingers, the stretch marks curving over her hips. She knew that he treasured every part of her, as much as she treasured every part of him. They were who they were. Neither of them would have it any other way.

She arced up into him as he nipped his way down her body. He was always so careful, so exquisitely careful, with those sharp-edged teeth. But tonight they scraped just a little harder, teasing, tormenting. She gasped as he pressed them into the soft flesh of her inner thigh, anticipation flooding her core.

"Now, Finn," she begged, winding her legs around him, offering herself up to his hungry mouth.

But still, he didn't bite. Oh, he claimed her with his mouth all right, until she writhed against him and screamed out his name, pleasure pounding through her louder than the waves. Yet he *still* didn't bite.

Spreading her legs wider, he pulled her upright, so that she straddled his lap. She cried out in wordless satisfaction as he slid into her. Slowly, so slowly, his bared teeth clenched with the effort of holding himself back. *She* bit at him, near-blind with need, but he didn't relent. He made her wait, his calloused hands hard on her hips, as he gave himself to her inch by exquisite inch.

At last, he filled her utterly. She trembled around him, held right on the brink of ecstasy, an excitement more intense than any she'd ever known singing through her veins. His shoulders were hard as iron under her hands, his breathing ragged. She knew he was a hairsbreadth away from losing all control, and just the thought of that nearly tipped her over the edge all on its own.

His eyes were just a ring of silver around deep, dark pupils. Feather-light, he kissed her lips, then worked his way down her neck. She whimpered with every touch of his mouth, clenching around him.

And still he didn't bite.

He rested his mouth right on the junction of her neck and shoulder. "Martha," he breathed.

"Finn." She tipped her head back for him, giving him her throat. "My mate."

The sharp points of his teeth pressed down. And he was in her and she was around him and at last, *at last*, they were one.

He was her mate, and she was his. And they would never be separated again.

"Will it leave a scar?" she asked him sleepily, much later.

His rough lips brushed tenderly against the shallow bite-mark, already scabbing over. "I think so."

She stretched happily, watching the horizon lighten with the first rays of dawn. "Good."

He chuckled, moving above her to claim her mouth again. *My mate,* he said softly, mind-to-mind.

Oh, his voice was beautiful in her soul. Deep and rich and strong as the sea. She would never tire of hearing the music of his true, secret self.

My mate, she said back, reflecting that pure, endless love.

Her stomach chose to break the moment by growling loudly. She groaned, covering her face in embarrassment, as Finn's shoulders shook in his dry, silent laugh.

"Oh Lord. Well, that certainly brings us back to reality with a bump." She sat up, brushing sand from her hair. "We'd better swim back home and find some breakfast."

He quirked an eyebrow at her. "It occurs to me…there is an excellent buffet on the other side of the island. It would be a much shorter swim. And we *did* cut our vacation short by a day."

"Oh, no, we can't just turn up at the resort unannounced, without even a reservation." She bit her lip, tempted despite herself. "Can we?"

"There are certain advantages to being a shark," he said, holding out his hand. His gray eyes gleamed wickedly. "No one expects me to observe social niceties."

Laughing, she let him pull her to her feet. Hand-in-hand, they headed for the sea, their footprints side-by-side in the white, eternally shifting sands.

<<<<>>>>

Printed in Great Britain
by Amazon